The Man in the Moone
and Other Early
Science Fiction Tales

www.firestonebooks.com

The Man in the Moone
and Other Early Science Fiction Tales

2012 Edition
Published by Firestone Books

Translation copyright © Firestone Books
Edited by David Lear

ISBN: 978-1-909608-06-1

Printed and bound by CreateSpace, USA

www.firestonebooks.com

You can also find out more by following Firestone Books on Facebook and Twitter

Contents

Introduction

Many people could be forgiven for thinking that concepts such as voyages into space, time travel, robots and extraterrestrials started in the nineteenth century with the works of Jules Verne, HG Wells and other science fiction pioneers. In truth, however, these ideas have far earlier origins, dating back a thousand years and more.

The beginnings of science fiction are hard, if not impossible to date. The Indian epic tale *Ramayana*, for instance, written around 500BC, tells of flying vehicles that could travel into space, but the story as a whole is fantasy with only a grain of science fiction. Going to the other extreme, it could be said that science fiction didn't begin until the mid-nineteenth century with the works of Jules Verne, whose tales were often founded on up-to-date science and futuristic technology.

For this collection of science fiction we have decided to cast the net widely and include stories which, while they may not be purely of this genre, are of historical interest and do contain at least some science fiction. For the purpose of this book we have started with Cicero's *Dream of Scipio*, written around 51BC, and our collection ends with Francis Godwin's *The Man in the Moone*, first published in 1638.

There is a break in European science fiction of around fifteen hundred years, from the decline of the

Greek and Roman cultures, until the beginning of the seventeenth century. This hibernation and subsequent reawakening had a number of causes:

During the dark ages there was a scarcity of written works in general. In medieval times the idea of life on other planets was viewed by many as heresy, so it is quite likely that writers judiciously avoided such subject matter.

In terms of the rebirth of science fiction, there were numerous factors, such as the declining power of the Church, and the advent of the printing press. There was also the circumnavigation of the Earth, meaning the world, which once must have seemed to have endless oceans and unlimited possibilities, now appeared to be a smaller and less interesting place. This meant fantasy writers had to look beneath the waves, underground, and out into space, for backdrops to their exotic tales.

The greatest influence on the pioneers of this genre however, was the rise of modern science, where the mysteries of life and the universe, were explained by observation and reason, rather than by supernatural belief. Writers who wished to create believable fantasy could no longer employ magic in their tales, and instead turned to speculative technology – the basis of much science fiction to this day.

Editor's Note

All the tales in this collection have been given their own brief introduction and, with the exception of *The Man in the Moone*, all the stories have been newly translated. *The Man in the Moone* has had its spelling and punctuation modernized, and also has a glossary that explain many archaic terms.

A point to note is the seven hundred year void between *The Tale of the Bamboo Cutter* (written circa 900) and *The Man in the Moone* (1638). Early science fiction stories were still being written during that time, for instance *Awaj bin Anfaq*, written circa 1250, by Al-Qazwini, and *Theologus Autodidactus* (c.1275) by Ibn al-Nafis. If we are able to find copies of stories such as these in the near future, and judge them to be of sufficient merit, we may include them in future volumes.

We had also hoped to publish a portion of *Somnium* (1634) by Johannes Kepler – a novel viewed by Carl Sagan and Isaac Asimov as being the first genuine science fiction tale. Again, if we are able to find a copy of this work, Firestone Books may publish a portion of the tale, or even the entire novel some time in the future.

The Dream of Scipio

Cicero

Introduction

Marcus Tullius Cicero (106BC–43BC) was a Roman philosopher, statesman and lawyer who, after a power struggle with Mark Anthony, was declared an enemy of the state and consequently murdered in 43BC.

The Dream of Scipio was written in 51BC, and is a fictional tale of General Scipio Aemilianus, a real person who lived 185BC–129BC. In the tale, Scipio's dream takes him into space where he meets his dead ancestors, and where he also views the Moon, Sun, stars and planets. He also sees how insignificant the Earth, the Roman Empire and human life are when compared with the majesty of the Universe. As to whether or not Scipio's soul actually ascended into space, or if it was simply a dream, is never revealed.

The Dream of Scipio

Cicero

When I was posted to Africa to serve as military tribune to the Fourth Legion, under General Manilius, I thought I might use the opportunity to pay a visit to King Masinissa, who had been a friend of the family for many years.

I travelled to his home and was escorted to his room where the old king embraced me and, to my surprise, began to cry.

"Praise be to the Sun and the Heavens," he wept. "Young Scipio has managed to pay me a visit before I depart from this life. Scipio – the mere mentioning of your name makes me feel young again. Looking at you now I can see so much of your grandfather, Africanus, in you. I don't need to tell you what a brilliant and fearless man he was, I'm sure."

After his kind words, we sat down and talked both of my Republic and his Kingdom. We had much to say, and the conversation was so interesting that the evening seemed to come all too quickly.

We ate and were soon after treated to the most spectacular entertainment, but instead of retiring to bed afterwards we continued our conversation. King Masinissa told me tales of my grandfather's exploits that I had never heard until now, and he imparted many wise words that my grandfather had, long ago, told him.

Eventually, the desire for sleep began to overwhelm us both and we were compelled to make our separate ways to bed. I shared a room with Laelius and others who were already slumbering, and after my long journey, and having stayed up so late, I quickly fell to sleep.

I have no doubt that all that we see and hear during the day, and preceding days, influence our dreams, and this night I soon found myself floating among the stars, and staring at someone familiar, but whose identity I could not fathom at first.

At last, as my earliest memories were trawled and I recalled a painting I had seen in my childhood, I realized I was face-to-face with my grandfather, Africanus. My blood chilled and I could not help but shudder.

"Do not be afraid, Scipio," my grandfather reassured. "I am here to help you, so listen carefully to all I say, and make sure you remember all I have said when you wake."

We were floating far above the Earth, and my grandfather pointed.

"You see that city?"

"Carthage?" I asked.

"Yes," he replied. "Long ago I used an army to conquer that town, and I made sure that they submitted to the will of the Roman people, but over time the citizens there have started to become restless. You in your capacity as a private soldier will soon be sent there to attack Carthage, and within two years you, as

Consul, will destroy that city. After that you will be made Censor, and you will embark on missions across Egypt, Syria, Asia Minor and Greece. During your your absence from the Roman Republic, your homeland, you will be elected as Consul a second time. With your growing power, you will bring an end to a most important war, and you will raze Numantia to the ground."

I was pleased to hear that my future sounded so fabulous, but before I could tell my grandfather, he warned me.

"You must at all times be aware of my other grandson, Tiberius. He is a schemer, and you would do well to keep your eye on him. When you eventually return to the Capitol, you will find the Republic greatly troubled by his evil ways. It is for you to save the Republic from him, and to do this, you must use all your courage and intelligence. As to whether or not you will be successful, I cannot say. After this point the future becomes shrouded in fog, through which I cannot see.

"At this time all the people of the Republic will look to you as the one man who can save them. Before reforming the Constitution – which is vital for you to do – you must first escape the murderous intentions of people close to you."

Laelius cried out in his sleep, causing our slumbering companions to groan loudly. I was almost ripped out of my dream.

"Be quiet," I murmured. "Please – let me stay in my dream."

My grandfather continued to speak as though there

had been no interruption.

"Reforming the Constitution for the good of the Republic is imperative, and if you do this you will be rewarded. Let me tell you now, Scipio, that every man who defends, expands or enriches the Republic, will be given a place in Heaven, where they may join their loved ones, and live with them in peace and happiness for all eternity.

"Nothing pleases the gods of the Universe more than seeing men coming together and being as one, united in one empire and under one set of common laws. The rulers of these states, though some may not even know it, are sent from Heaven to rule over their people, and will return to Heaven once their bodies die."

Despite the idea that for all the good deeds I'd done I might find my way to Heaven, I still felt uneasy – not because I was reminded of my mortality, but because someone close might kill me.

I asked my grandfather if, though his body was long dead, he was in fact still alive.

"Yes," he replied.

"And what about all those other people I had thought lost forever when they died – are they here now? What about my father?"

"Yes, Scipio," he smiled. "They are all here, alive and well. When their mortal bodies failed them, they were released from their Earthly chain and able to fly away to Heaven. Look, Scipio. See who is approaching. It is your father, Paulus!"

I turned and could scarcely believe my eyes. My father had come, and I was unable to hold back my tears. He embraced me, and kissed me, and told me to dry my eyes.

It was some time before I was able to stem the tearful flow, and after I had regained my composure I was just able to speak.

"Father, you were the best and noblest parent I could have wished for," I said.

He reciprocated the compliment, and I asked him, "If life on Earth is little more than death, while true life is here in Heaven among the ones I love, shouldn't I end my Earthly life as soon as I return there?"

My father shook his head.

"That is not the way of the Universe," he explained. "Unless the god of all that surrounds us releases you from your body, entry to this higher place will be forbidden. The same rule applies to all men. No one can hasten his own entry to Heaven by taking his own life. All men are made from those everlasting fires you call stars, spherical fires that orbit the Earth at great speed and each of which possesses its own divine intelligence, and all men are guardians of the globe that lies in the middle of the Heavens – the Earth. If you end your own life, you will be seen as deserting the post that was assigned to you. Only the god of all may decide how and when your mortal body shall die.

"While you are on Earth, you must be a man who is both pious and just, as I was, and your grandfather before me. The state will always take on the qualities of its people, and if you are noble and just, you will benefit the Republic. This then is the way into Heaven. Here you will be reunited those you loved and had once thought lost, in the place they call the Milky Way."

I gazed at all the Heavenly bodies that surrounded me, and among the fires of Heaven I saw a brilliant ring of light – the Milky Way.

I saw stars that could not be seen from Earth, and their size was almost beyond my comprehension. Of all the Heavenly bodies, the smallest was the Moon, reflecting the Sun's brilliant light. The Earth too was dwarfed by the stars, and suddenly man and all his follies and adventures and discoveries seemed insignificant. I suddenly felt embarrassed and ashamed that the Republic's mighty empire was an insignificant dot on a tiny planet.

My grandfather must have caught my gaze. "Come," he said. "Do not fixate upon the Earth. Let us look around the Heavens together."

He pointed and I followed the line of his finger. "See how the Universe is made of nine circles or, more accurately, nine spheres," he explained. "The outermost of these is the supreme deity embedded with stars, the Heavenly sphere that contains all others. Within this are seven spheres that orbit the Earth in contrary motion to the stars. The first sphere is Saturn, while the next, Jupiter, is a god-like place that gives hope and good health to mankind. Next is the Sun – ruler of all things luminous and is of such size that it gives everything in the system light. Next are Venus and Mercury, following the Sun as it moves. Last of all, and nearest the Earth, orbits the Moon, lit by the rays of the Sun.

While the Moon shall last forever, what lies beneath, on Earth, is doomed to wither and die. Only souls that the gods have given to mankind are eternal.

Earth, orbited by the planets and stars, lies at the heart of the Universe. It does not move, and all things of mass tend towards it."

I looked in awe at these immense globes as they orbited, and for the first time I was able to discern a sweet sound.

"What is that beautiful harmony that I can hear?" I asked.

"It is the sound of the planets," my father replied. "Each body in the Universe produces a sound, like a musical note, as it moves. Those objects furthest from the Earth produce higher notes, those closest produce the bass notes, and together they produce the most beautiful harmony."

"But I have never heard this sound before," I said, "and I have never read of it."

"There is no duller sense than that of hearing," said my father, "and men's ears, to some degree, have been deafened by this sound so they are unable to hear it."

The Heavens were a truly wondrous place, with the Moon and Sun, the planets and stars. But still, in spite of all the beauty and majesty of Heaven, I could not help but gaze once more towards the Earth.

"I see you are still thinking about the world that is your home," said my father. "When you return, and look back up into the night sky, you will realize how small and insignificant the Earth really is. It is only right you should think this, for it is the truth. You would also do well to realize, that compared to the size of the Earth, the Republic is barely a speck.

"Look Scipio. See how there are only a few pockets of civilization, surrounded by great swathes of emptiness. The size of these barren areas is so great that communication between these islands of civilization is impossible.

"If you seek glory, your fame might spread through the Republic – but for how long? The other pockets of human beings will never hear of you. Your fame will never be that great, when you look at the Earth as a whole. See how your planet is divided into zones white with ice in the north and south, a hot belt encompassing the middle of the Earth, and two habitable zones between the equator and each of the poles. Look at those men who inhabit the inhabitable zone in the south. They walk upside down, and their affairs will never concern you, and they will forever be oblivious to any so-called glory that you might achieve.

"If you climbed the Caucasus or swam across the Ganges, who beyond that tiny speck of an Empire would hear and celebrate your name? Ask yourself also for how long would your name be remembered? Your glory, like all glory, will surely fade away. To begin with, your children and grandchildren might celebrate all you have done, but in time your descendants will be as ignorant of your achievements as your ancestors.

"Just as the Republic is little more than a point on a small planet, so the time-scales you are familiar with are, in reality, fleeting moments. To you, a year is the time it takes for the Sun to return to its point of origin, but this is not quite so. A true year, a Heavenly measurement of time, occurs when all Heavenly bodies, stars and all, have gone through a full revolution and returned to their original points. How many generations come and go, I can scarcely imagine. Now you should have some sense of space and time on a cosmic scale."

"I understand," I replied. "Even if it is almost beyond my comprehension."

"If you wish to ascend to Heaven after your life ends," said my grandfather, "do not spend your life on Earth seeking out glory, or material possessions, or enslaving yourself to the opinions and whims of others. Do not be consumed by what others think and say about you. Rise above their cruel words. No matter how hard you try to appease them, they will always talk. Be pious, and just, and virtuous. These should be your aims while you walk the Earth, not so that you can get into Heaven, but because good deeds should be done for their own sake."

"Now that you have told me all this," I said, "I will try even harder to follow in your footsteps and those of my father. I hope I will fare well, and hope you will both be able to watch me from Heaven."

"Keep along the path you have already been following and you will not go wrong. Remember always that while your body will one day cease, your soul is immortal. You are a god Scipio; one that feels, acts and thinks, has memory and prescience, who is master of his physical body, just as the god of all moves the Universe.

"Spend your life in the pursuit of the noblest activities, doing what you can for your country, and putting others before yourself. Do this and your soul will be welcomed all the more into the Kingdom of

Heaven. Do not give yourself over to the pleasures of the flesh, and do not give in to whims and desires – this is to go against the laws of the gods and of fellow men. If you succumb to such temptations, your soul will spend many ages wandering unhappily upon the Earth, before finally being allowed into Heaven."

My grandfather faded before my very eyes, until he was nothing, and then I awoke from my dream.

True History

Lucian of Samosata

Introduction

Lucian of Samosata (125–c.180) was a Greek satirist of Syrian or Assyrian extraction, and *True History* is perhaps his most well-known tale. This piece of fantastical fiction parodies many works such as Homer's *Odyssey*, and is certainly a contender for the title of earliest science fiction story. In the first half of *True History*, the protagonist visits the Moon, meets extraterrestrial creatures, and takes part in interplanetary warfare.

In this second part the protagonist sails the ocean, visits strange islands, and meets Homer and Herodotus during his travels. In the end he tells of reaching a continent that he wishes to explore, and says he will relate his continuing adventures in a following volume. No such volume is known to exist, and so what happened to the character after this point is uncertain.

True History

Lucian of Samosata

Book 1

Athletes train on a regular basis, and no doubt look forward to taking a break from their exertions. Similarly, students who spend their time pouring over their academic texts, enjoy resting and thinking about more pleasurable things. While it might be tempting to spend time reading humorous texts, students might also wish to read something that is not only funny, but thought-provoking, and hopefully this book is just the thing.

I hope the readers will enjoy the humour and novelty of this book, and enjoy the lies that are woven together in what I hope is a believable way. I hope too that the reader will be amused by my parodies of poets, historians and philosophers.

No doubt the reader will recognize many of those whom I seek to imitate, but I will mention two of those whose work has influenced this book. Firstly I will mention Ctesias, who wrote fantastic tales about India without ever having been there. Secondly I wish to mention Iambulus who also wrote much that was untrue, but whose writings are all the more fun for the fantasies they contain.

Many have written of having visited lands that, in fact, do not exist, or at least do not exist outside their imaginations, and whose aim is to deceive gullible people. The man who first inspired this deceit was Homer's Odysseus, with his tales of one-eyed men, many-headed animals, cannibals, and the transformations of his drug-addled sailors. I do not blame people for writing such fantasies, but it does amaze me how they expect others to believe such blatant nonsense.

I have been eager for some time to write a story of my life, but my autobiography would make for a very dull read. So I have decided instead to do what many have done before, and write the most fantastic work of fiction my mind can create.

I shall differ from these other writers by acknowledging that everything I put to paper is nothing more than a series of lies. Nothing in this book is based on my life or the life of anyone I have known. It is a work of complete fiction, and no one should believe a word of what is written in this fantastical tale:

Many years ago, I began to wonder what land lay at the end of the Atlantic Ocean and, if such a place existed, what kind of strange beings might live there. At first this thought flitted idly through my mind, but soon this mild curiosity grew to something that continually gnawed at me, and in the end I felt compelled to seek out the answer myself.

I was fortunate enough to be the owner of a fine ship, and so had the means to satisfy my inquisitive mind. I filled the ship with plenty of fresh water, a good store of food, a great quantity of weapons, fifty crew whom I knew and trusted, and who shared my desire for adventure and knowledge, and I enlisted the finest sailing master money could induce.

We set forth across the Mediterranean, and with a fair wind behind us we passed through the Pillars of Hercules and out into the Atlantic Ocean. For the first day and night the wind calmed until there was not even the faintest gust. We barely travelled and looking back, the Pillars of Hercules remained quite visible.

On the second day however, the sun rose and brought with it a gale. The sea swelled, and dark clouds rushed towards us until they had blotted out the whole sky. The wind buffeted us mercilessly, and was so strong and so ferocious that we were unable to bring our sails in. At the mercy of the elements, we could do nothing but let ourselves be swept along, and for seventy nine helpless days the wind blew us across the ocean. On the eightieth day however, the storm abated, and the clouds broke up to reveal the sun once more.

With the darkness finally vanquished, I was able to make out a tree-covered island, some leagues away.

Still weak and weary from our months of hardship, we weighed anchor close to the shore, and rested ourselves on the beach. After lying on the sand for some hours, weary and miserable at our situation, I rose to my feet and commanded thirty crew to stay and guard our ship, while I led the rest of the crew on an expedition across the island.

We tramped into the wood, and after half a mile we

came to a clearing where we found a great slab of weathered bronze with an inscription. The writing was not altogether clear as the slab had turned green with age and the letters were faint or obliterated. After a careful examination, we were able to piece together the message:

"Hercules and Dionysus made it no further than this point" it read.

One of my men pointed out two giant sets of footprints, pressed deep in the earth. One must have been a hundred feet in length, and the other was smaller but still far beyond the size of an ordinary man. The larger print, I did not doubt, belonged to Hercules, and the smaller to Dionysus.

We gave our salutations to these two great beings, and continued with our exploration of the island. We had not had a drop to drink for so long that when we came across a river that cut through the wood, we knelt down gratefully and drank from it. To our surprise the river was not made of water, however, but of wine.

I decided to seek out the source of this strange river, and we followed it upstream. What we found were grapevines laden with fruit. From the roots of each vine came a stream of clear wine, and these streams came together to form the river.

Fish swam about under the surface, similar in colour to the wine. We caught and ate some of these fish and became drunk as a result, so we ate other fish we had brought with us on our expedition to mitigate the effects.

After eating, we pushed forwards once more, but

had not gone far when we came upon a wondrous sight. Some of the grapevines had trunks that were healthy and stout, but the upper part of each was a woman, perfectly formed from the waist up. Indeed, they reminded me of the pictures I had seen of Daphne turning into a tree just as Apollo catches her. The hair on each lady's head was made of leaves and tendrils, and from their fingertips grew branches full of grapes.

They welcomed us in a variety of languages; Indian and Lydian, but mostly Greek. They kissed some of my men on the lips, and those who were kissed instantly became drunk. The ladies would not let us take their fruit, and cried out in pain if we plucked a grape. Some of the women looked upon my men with hungry eyes, and asked if my crew might embrace them. Two men ventured forward and wrapped their arms about these strange creatures, but the moment they did so they found themselves stuck; their lower bodies had grown thick roots, their hair had turned to leaves and tendrils, and they were already beginning to bear fruit like the women.

Nothing could be done to break this strange spell so, leaving our two unfortunate men, we returned to the ship and recounted our adventure to the rest of the crew. We filled barrels with fresh water and wine from the island, and camped on the beach overnight.

As the sun rose and was barely above the horizon, we boarded our ship and set sail. The wind picked up with every hour, and I heard a crew member shout fearfully and point. In the distance a waterspout rose from the sea and reached high into the sky, far above any clouds. In a restless manner it twisted and bent, and moved towards us in a most ominous manner.

I called for the crew to set sail away as quickly as possible from this phenomenon, but it gained ground with every minute, until at last we were lashed by its watery coil and we were forced to brace ourselves. The boat was sucked upwards, mile after mile. For seven days and nights we sailed through the sky and through a fog of clouds until, at last, we were let down on a strange land that was bright and round and shining a brilliant light.

Surveying the landscape, there were islands and water, and we soon saw that the islands were inhabited and cultivated. In the sky we say great flying creatures heading towards us, and as they approached, we saw that they were men flying on three-headed vultures. The great birds landed in front of us and the men dismounted. They said they were the king's Vulture Soldiers, and told us that we were all under arrest. The leader of the Vulture Soldiers explained that it was the job of his men to fly about the country and bring any strangers they might find to the court of the king.

We were escorted to the king's palace where the king surveyed us all curiously, not least the clothes we wore.

"You are Greeks, are you not?" he said.

"We are," I replied.

He looked at me puzzled, and shook his head. "How did you get here – when there is nothing but air between our two worlds?"

"A waterspout whipped up my boat," I explained. "It carried us for seven days and seven nights before depositing us here."

The king nodded. "My name is Endymion," he said, "and I too am from your country. I was brought here in a dream and was made king of this world that by night shines down upon your Earth. You are standing on the Moon."

He pointed through a window, and in the night sky we saw a world with rivers and seas, forests and mountains and cities. It was our world, Earth.

"You have no need to fear us," said the king. "You are in no danger, and I will ensure all your needs are met. And if I am victorious in my war with the people of the Sun, then you can share in my success and lead the happiest of lives in my world."

"Who are these people of the Sun?" I asked. "And why do you fight them?"

"Years ago," said the king, "I decided to gather together the poorest people on my world, and use them to set up a colony on Venus – a world that is currently uninhabited. But Phaethon, King of the Sun, sent his Ant Soldiers out to thwart our colonization. We were forced to retreat, for we were no match for them. But now we are stronger, and I desire to make war with the people of the Sun, and again establish a colony on Venus. If you wish, you and your men can join me in battle. I will give you a uniform and a royal vulture, and we shall set off together tomorrow."

I nodded. "My men and I will join you."

We stayed the night as guests of the king, and noticed that there were no women upon the Moon, only men, and indeed the king confirmed this. I would have asked many questions, but my men and I needed to rest, so we slept as best we could, and the next morning we prepared for battle.

My men and I, seated on our vultures, took our place among the strangest array of creatures. There were eighty thousand mounted Vulture Soldiers; there were birds with grass plumage and lettuce-leaf wings; there were giant fleas that had travelled from the Great Bear constellation with archers on their backs, and a host of other fabulous beasts.

Giant spiders, the size of islands, were told by the king to weave a web between the Moon and Venus. What the spiders actually wove was a thick plane extending like a bridge between both worlds, and some sixty million men were deployed on it.

All the soldiers, including myself, were attired with armour made from lupine skins, helmets hollowed out from tough beans, and we were given swords and shields emblazoned with Greek patterns.

A scout warned that the enemy was approaching, and sure enough we saw Phaethon, King of the Sun, coming towards us with his equally strange army. There were some fifty thousand Ant Soldiers, each ant being some two hundred feet long; fifty thousand archers mounted on giant mosquitoes; beings who fired deadly radishes; Mushroom Men who used mushrooms as shields and asparaguses as spears, and dog-faced men who had flown from the Dog Star on winged acorns. The Sun King was supposed to have been joined by the formidable Cloud Centaurs, but as the enemy approached us the Cloud Centaurs were nowhere to be seen. Finally there were the donkeys who began to bray, and so signalled the start of the battle.

The Vulture Soldiers, myself included, rushed forwards only to see the whole of the Sun King's left flank flee. We pursued them without letting up, until at last we caught them and were able to cut them down.

Their right flank faired much better, with their mosquitoes very much on the offensive. Only when our infantry joined the battle did the mosquitoes finally retreat, and when they saw their left flank had been annihilated, they turned and fled.

It was a swift and glorious victory. We took many prisoners, and an even greater number were slain. So much blood poured onto the clouds beneath us that they turned crimson, just like when the sun sets. Indeed, I wonder if this is what happened when, as Homer mentioned, after the death of Sarpedon, Zeus turned the rain into blood.

All the soldiers of the Moon King celebrated routing the enemy. The infantry celebrated upon the giant spider web, while the rest of us who had fought in the great sky battle alighted on clouds and bathed in our victory.

Our celebrations were premature. Scouts came to us in a state of panic – the Cloud Centaurs who had not arrived to help the King of the Sun before battle were now fast approaching. I looked up and saw shapes, indistinct at first, approaching at great speed. Most of the Moon King's men had not even noticed the spectacle, and we were ill-prepared for another fight. The Cloud Centaurs were a sight to behold. They were winged horses, but with the upper bodies of men. These were massive creatures – from the waist up each man was as large as the Colossus of Rhodes.

Their leader was the Archer from the Zodiac, and when they saw their allies had been defeated, they sent word to Phaethon telling him to advance again. Before the people of the Moon were able to regroup for battle, the Cloud Centaurs swooped down and attacked. The Moon King's soldiers were either slain or put to flight, and even those who fled were caught and cut down. Endymion, the King of the Moon, was pursued back to the Moon's capital, where most of his birds were killed. My men and I were chased across the spider's web, and I was captured along with two of my companions.

Our hands were tied behind our backs, bound by thread from the spiders' web, and we were taken to the Sun. The Sun King decided not to lay siege to the Moon, but instead to build a wall in the air so that the rays of the Sun should no longer reach the Moon. The Wall was not made of stone, but of cloud, and the Moon was completely shrouded in darkness.

Endymion sent a message to Phaethon, begging the King of the Sun to tear down the wall and let the Moon be flooded with light once more. In return for this, the King of the Moon promised to pay the King of the Sun money in perpetuity, to become an ally of the Sun People, never to make war again, and suggested they swap all the hostages that they had captured.

At first Phaethon and his Sun People were still incensed by the war-like ways of Endymion and the People of the Moon, and they would not countenance any sort of treaty. But, in time, their feelings and their position softened, and they sent the Moon People their terms for peace:

The People of the Sun and their allies shall make a treaty with the People of the Moon, under the following conditions:

– Each world shall exchange all prisoners captured during their war

– The Sun People shall pull down the wall of cloud that blocks the light to the Moon

– The Sun People shall never again invade the Moon

– The Moon People shall never invade the Sun

– Each world shall aid the other if either one comes under attack

– The Moon People shall allow all stars and planets to remain autonomous

– The King of the Moon shall send the King of the Sun ten thousand gallons of dew as tribute, and give ten thousand of his men over as hostages

– The colonization of Venus shall be carried out concurrently by both the Moon People and the Sun People, and any others who wish to do so

– This treaty shall be inscribed on a slab that will be positioned equidistantly between worlds

The treaty was signed by three officials from the Sun and three from the Moon, and on these terms peace was made. The cloud-wall was dismantled and my two men and I, who were still prisoners, were released and allowed to return to the Moon.

When we reached our destination, Endymion himself greeted us, as did our old crew mates who wept with happiness.

Endymion, who was overjoyed at our return, kindly offered me his son's hand in marriage. He could not persuade me however, and in the end he had to accept my decision. I asked him that I be allowed to return to my homeland, along with my crew. Endymion reluctantly agreed, but he asked me to stay another week, which I did.

Those days were among the strangest I can recount, such are the ways of the People of the Moon. There are no women on the Moon, and they had not even heard of the word. It is a place where men marry men, and men give birth to children. Before the age of twenty-five men act as wives, and thereafter they assume the role of husband.

I saw that pregnant men did not carry their unborn babies in their stomachs, but in their calves. Conception does not take place as one might expect – instead each man has a hole in the hollow of his knee. After the act, the man's calf will gradually begin to swell, until the baby is ready for delivery. When it is due, the calf is cut and the baby is taken out, quite dead, then a Moon Person will gently breathe life into the baby's mouth.

If this sounds unusual then I shall tell you another

way they go about procreating that is even more fantastic. They have beings called Arboreals who are brought about through a most unusual process. A man's right testicle is cut off, and then planted in the ground. Over time it grows into a large tree made of flesh. It is shaped like a giant phallus, and when I first saw such a tree, it reminded me of the tale of Priapus. The tree has branches and leaves, and eventually bears fruit in the form of giant acorns. When the fruit eventually ripen, they are harvested. Men cut them down from the trees, slice them open, and inside the giant acorns are the men who, as already mentioned, are called Arboreals.

Another unusual aspect with regards Moon People, is that they have artificial phalluses. The rich have phalluses of ivory or other expensive materials, while the poor generally have phalluses of wood which are used during intercourse.

When a man grows old and dies, he does not become a corpse, instead he gradually turns to vapour and becomes at one with the air.

All Moon People eat the same food, namely frogs. These amphibians do not hop around but instead fly through the air, and are caught and cooked on hot coals. While the frogs are roasting, the natives sit about the fire and inhale the smoke that rises, before finally consuming their meal.

Their favoured drink is also very peculiar – it is the air, which is quite liquid and is squeezed into cups like dew. They also never need to relieve themselves and they do not have the necessary bodily parts to do so.

Any man on the Moon is considered beautiful if he

has not the slightest scrap of hair on his head, and any person with long hair is reckoned to be quite hideous. People who live on comets, however, hold the opposite view, and consider anyone with long hair to be quite beautiful.

Moon People have a great number of unusual aspects to their bodies, which are quite dissimilar to our own. Adult Moon People have beards that grow not from their chins, but from their knees. They have only one toe on each foot, and no toenails. Each man has a cabbage-leaf tail that hangs and covers his buttocks, and never breaks even if he falls on his behind. When their noses run, honey of great pungency pours from their nostrils. When they work hard or take exercise, milk sweats from their bodies. The milk is of such quality that, with the addition of a little honey, it can be made into a quite delicious cheese.

They use their bellies as pockets, and can open and shut these pouches. Inside their bellies there appear to be no intestines, instead I have only ever noticed hair, and during colder periods the children are able to climb into these pouches and keep warm.

If I tell you the amazing properties of their eyes, you will most probably think I am a very great liar. Nevertheless, I shall take that risk:

Their eyes are not fixed in their skulls, but can be plucked out of their sockets. If they have no need to see anything, they frequently take their eyes out and stow them away. Then, when the need arises, they retrieve their eyes and put them back in. If a person should happen to lose his own eyes, he will simply borrow another person's so that he can see once more. The wealthier class of people always keep a large stock of eyes.

The Moon's citizens generally have leaves for ears. Those who do not are the Arboreals who instead have ears made of wood.

From onions they extract oil which is clear and sweet-smelling like myrrh. They have water-grapes that resemble hailstones. When the wind blows, the grapevines are shaken, and the result is that these hailstones come loose and tumble down to Earth.

When it comes to clothes, the rich wear garments made from a soft and malleable glass, while the poor wear clothes spun from bronze, which is first turned into a wool-like substance by soaking it in water.

I was walking across the royal grounds when I came across a large, angled mirror, fixed above a well. I was told that any person looking into the mirror can see every country and every city on Earth, just as if he was flying over it. If a person descends this shallow well they can hear every word that is spoken on the planet below.

I peered into this strange looking-glass, and was able to see my family and my native land, though I am unable to say if they were able to see me.

I know I have made an astonishing series of claims, but any doubter, if he reaches the Moon himself, will know that I am speaking the truth.

So these seven days of observing the Moon and the people who lived there passed, and it was time for me and my men to bid farewell to the king and the other Moon People whom we had befriended.

Endymion gave me two tunics made of glass, five of bronze, and a suit of lupine armour. These gifts and more were placed on our ship, and we set sail from the Moon, escorted some sixty miles by a thousand Vulture Soldiers. After they left us and returned to the Moon, we passed many places on our voyage, but we did not stop until we reached Venus. The world was already being colonized by people from the Moon and the Sun. We rested there awhile, and filled our barrels with their water.

We returned to our ship and set off once more, travelling towards the Zodiac. Our journey took us past the Sun. Many of the crew wished to pay a visit to the Sun, but owing to unfavourable winds we were sadly unable. We did at least pass close enough by to see that the lands were green and lush and well kept. Something we hadn't bargained for however were the Cloud Centaurs, who on seeing us flew up towards our ship. Without the Vulture Soldiers protection, I feared there might be another bloody battle. Fortunately we were able to head off any skirmish by showing them the peace treaty, and the Cloud Centaurs left us in peace.

Sailing for another night and day, beginning our slow descent to Earth, we came across a city floating between the constellations of Pleiades and Hyades. This was the City of Light. We landed and toured the town. Here we found no men, only flaming torches. We saw them running down streets, relaxing in the public square, or waiting down at the harbour. Some torches were small and scruffy, while a few were large, powerful and conspicuous.

Each torch had his own house or sconce, each torch had his own name, and we even heard them talking. As a gesture of goodwill we were invited into their homes, but we were distrustful of them and we neither ate a morsel that was offered to us, or slept the night.

In the centre of their city, there was a public building, where the city's judge sat. He would call each torch by name, and any torch that did not answer his call was sentenced to death for desertion. The method of execution was by extinguishing. My crew and I even visited the court and watched the proceedings. Here we saw torches defending themselves, and explaining why they had come so late.

It was in the court that I came across a familiar figure – my own flaming torch. We talked for a while, and he told me about his home life.

After this fleeting reunion, my crew and I returned to the ship and set off once more. Again we found ourselves floating across the Earth's sky, and slowly downwards, until we were as low as the clouds. There was a city on one of the clouds but, as happened when we passed the Sun, the wind prevented us from paying the Cloud City a visit. As I looked down at the clouds I could not help but be reminded of Aristophanes' great play.

After another two days the ocean was in plain sight, but the only place we could land, given we were still high in the air, were floating lands that seemed fiery and bright.

Finally, the wind fell to a gentle breeze and we were able to touch down on the ocean. The weather was fine and the sea was calm, and in their happiness and excitement to have returned from our aerial travels the crew leapt overboard and swam happily in the water.

Unfortunately, it is often the case that a time of happiness is followed quickly by one of misery:

For two days we sailed in fair weather, and it was on the third day that one of the crew spotted a number of sea-monsters. The creatures were whales, the largest of which was a hundred and fifty miles long. As this mighty beast pushed towards us, his gargantuan mouth open, we had no chance of escape. Before he had reached us, the water he was displacing caused our ship to be thrown about violently, and turned much of the ocean to foam.

Every person on the boat believed himself doomed. We embraced and said our last goodbyes, and waited for death.

The monster's teeth were larger than great statues, white as ivory, and sharper than the jagged metal spines of caltrops. The water that the whale was swallowing pulled us unstoppably between his teeth, and then his mouth snapped shut, just missing our boat and leaving us in complete darkness.

We were thankful that we should still be alive, but our our ordeal was clearly not over. After some time in this dark void, the whale opened his mouth once more, and we were able to survey our surroundings.

We were in something resembling a great, domed cavern, large enough to house a great city. All about us there was water with all sorts of detritus floating about: there were the remains of fish both large and small, there was ships' rigging, anchors, merchandise, human bones, and the remains of creatures that I could not recognize.

In the middle of this great artificial lake was an island which, I imagine, had formed over time from all the mud the whale had swallowed. Trees had grown and covered much of the island, there were plants, and there was life, and it seemed clear to me that the island had been cultivated by intelligent minds.

We sailed about the coast of the island and found it to be twenty-seven miles in circumference. We also saw a great variety of birds in the trees, including seagulls and kingfishers.

When we weighed anchor and went ashore, many of my men could not help but cry and lament our miserable situation. I tried to rouse the crew, and suggested we light a fire to banish the darkness. We still had fish on board our ship, and we also had plenty of water that we had brought with us from Venus. After gathering what dry wood we could find, and rubbing two sticks together we were soon able to cook some fish over a blazing fire.

We slept soundly, and on waking the next day we were able to see the outside world in glimpses whenever the whale opened his great mouth. We might see mountains, then endless sky, and then islands, and we reasoned that he must be moving swiftly through the ocean.

As we were unsure if we would ever be able to escape from within this great beast, I took seven of my men into the forest, which I wished to explore. We had travelled close to a mile when, obscured by trees, we came across a temple. An inscription told us it had been dedicated to Poseidon, and on exploring the grounds around the temple we found a number of graves.

But there were livelier signs too. Nearby, there was a spring of clear water. In the distance we heard a dog barking, and venturing in that direction we first saw smoke, and then a farmhouse.

We made our way to the house, and saw a boy and an old man, hard at work watering their garden. They saw us but at first said nothing and we all stood in silence.

At last the old man spoke: "Who are you, strangers? Are you sea-gods, or unlucky men like us?"

"We are men," I replied.

The old man nodded. "We too are men, born on land. But given our situation we have become sea-creatures and swim with the creatures that surround our island. Sometimes I wonder if we now reside in the land of the dead, but sincerely hope that we are still alive."

"You are alive, sir," I reassured. "My men and I were swallowed, ship and all, by this great beast only yesterday. We came ashore on this island and decided to explore the forest and now, by some good fortune, have met other men who share our predicament in being imprisoned inside this whale. Pray tell us who you are and how you came to be trapped here like us."

But on both these points the old man remained silent, and beckoned us to follow him into his house.

His home was spacious and comfortable; there were bunk beds, and all sorts of other furniture. We sat ourselves down at a table, and the host laid out a meal of fish and fruit and vegetables, and poured us all goblets full of wine.

At last he spoke, but not of himself. "Tell me of your adventures that led you here."

I spoke at length of the storm that had blown us to the island with the strange female vines, of our trip to the Moon and the battles between the people of the Moon and of the Sun, and all the rest up to our being swallowed by the whale.

Our host was amazed by our adventures, and then he recounted his own tale:

"My name is Scintharus. I have not always lived in this great beast. Originally I hale from Cyprus. My boy, Cinyras, who is with us now, my servants, and I set sail from our native country in the hope of trading in Italy. For much of the journey our voyage was a pleasant one. But as we neared Sicily, the wind picked up and drove us far out into the ocean. It was during this storm that we were swallowed by the whale. Our ship was smashed and the only people to survive were myself and my son.

"We buried what crew happened to be washed up onto this island, and we built a temple to Poseidon, and live here now, surviving on vegetables and fish and nuts. The forest also contains many grape-vines, from which we derive our delicious wine, and we also have the spring that you no doubt saw.

"Our beds are made of leaves, we have more than enough wood to burn fires, and the fish and birds are plentiful in number and easy enough to catch. There is also a lake not too far from here. It's a few miles in circumference, with all kinds of fish swimming about under the surface. It's also a lovely place to swim, and

I have a small boat which my son and I use to sail.

"Twenty seven years have passed since we were swallowed, and our lives here would have been a tolerable one – if it was not for our neighbours."

My mouth dropped open. "You mean there are other people inside the whale?"

"Yes," Scintharus said grimly. "There are lots of them. But they are all unpleasant and quarrelsome. In the western part of the forest live the Lobster Men. They have eel-eyes, and faces like lobsters. They love nothing more than to pick a fight with anyone. There are also Fish Men who have the upper bodies of men and the lower bodies of catfish, and a host of other creatures that resemble both humans and sea creatures. I am forced to pay the tribute of five hundred oysters a year to some of these creatures, but I'm tired of it – it is no life."

I pitied the poor man and told him as much.

"Do you think," he asked, "that we might be able to wage war on these creatures? I have no doubt if they find out about you – which no doubt they will – they will expect tribute from you too."

"How many of them are there?" I asked.

"More than a thousand," Scintharus replied.

"What sort of weapons do they have?"

"Nothing at all, but for a few fish bones."

"Good," I said. "I think we have some chance. Hopefully they are unaware of our existence. We should meet them in battle, and quickly. We have superior weapons, and we will have the element of surprise."

The old man was heartened by my words, and I

went on:

"If we defeat them, then we can live out the rest of our lives in peace."

Our plan was to draw the enemy to us, rather than blunder into their territory of which we knew little. To this end, Scintharus did not pay the tribute when the time came, and a messenger was sent by one of the Fish Men demanding that the payment of five hundred oysters be made at once. Scintharus gave the messenger a contemptuous reply and chased him off.

The following day they sent some of their men to attack Scintharus and his son, but we were lying in wait and were able to cut the men down with ease. We chased after the few that escaped and followed them back to their den. After a short and glorious battle, we found ourselves victorious. The number of their dead was a hundred and seventy five, and the number of our dead was just one – our sailing-master, who had been run through with a sharpened fish-bone.

We celebrated through the night, but the next morning more of their men were sent and they knew now that there was more than just a man and his son to deal with. We met them outside the temple of Poseidon. Again we were able to rout them; their weapons were simply no match for ours, and, as before, we chased the enemy into the forest. This time they knew they were well and truly beaten, and now it was we, and not they, who were rulers of this island.

They sent men to take away their dead, and sent a party to discuss the formation of an alliance. We, however, thought it best not to engage in any sort of treaty and, the next day, we marched into their territory and killed every one of them – except for the Sea Goats who fled the scene and hurled themselves into the sea.

With the enemy vanquished or killed, we were all able to live in peace. It was a luxurious life in many ways where we were able to spend our time in leisurely pursuits such as hunting, sports, tending vines and gathering fruit. But for all this life of idle pleasure, it still troubled me that we were ultimately prisoners, cut off from the outside world by this great whale.

For a year and eight months we lived this life. But early during our ninth month, not long after the whale opened it's mouth, as it did on a regular basis, we heard a commotion. I heard what sounded like the drum-beats that sailors row to, and with my men I crossed the island towards the opening of the whale's mouth, and peered towards the outside world.

What we saw, we could scarcely believe. Huge men were rowing islands that were miles in circumference, using cypress trees as oars. The trees that covered the island had large leaves which together had the combined effect not dissimilar to a boat's sail.

At first there were only two or three, but soon more came into sight until I counted over six hundred islands. Their intentions soon became clear when some collided head-on, and a number were scuttled and sunk. The giants sometimes ran aboard an enemy's island and hand-to-hand battles took place. No quarter was given.

They struck at one another with massive oysters and with giant sponges. From what we were able to discern, the battle stemmed from one sides act of piracy, where herds of dolphins belonging to the other side were driven off. Eventually the victims of this piracy were the victors in battle, and the other side fled.

The remaining giants, tethered their islands to the whale, and were pulled along for the next day, before burying their fallen friends on the whale, then sailing away on their strange islands until they were beyond the horizon.

Book 2

I had become accustomed to living inside the whale, but upon seeing the outside world once more I felt discontented with this life and sought a way of escape. Our first attempt involved digging through the side of the whale, but after tunnelling more than half a mile we gave up. Our next plan was to set the forest alight and hopefully kill the whale. For a week we worked night and day, setting the forest ablaze, beginning near the tail, but it was only on the eighth and ninth days that the whale showed any symptoms of illness. He yawned less frequently, and his yawns did not last as long. On the tenth and eleventh days, we knew that the fires were really having an effect, and he made the most tremendous noises.

On the twelfth day we realized that if we did not prop open his mouth the next time he yawned, we might find ourselves stuck inside a dead whale and die there ourselves. Some crew took trees to the whale's mouth and waited. When he yawned, his mouth was propped open.

With Scintharus as our new sailing-master, we filled our boat with what provisions we were able to gather. One more day passed before the whale died, and we set off in our boat, making our way between the creature's teeth with some difficulty.

For three days we camped on the whale's back, and on the fourth day we set off in our boat. We sailed between the bodies of the dead giants, and upon measuring their bodies were amazed at their height.

We travelled in a northerly direction and as each day passed the climate cooled. Then, after a week of sailing, the north wind brought with it a great chill. The temperature plunged so much that the sea froze over, and our boat lay on top of a great sheet of ice that spread all about us as far as the eye could see.

The wind was so cold, we were barely able to stand it. Scintharus proposed that we dig a hole in the ice so that we might be sheltered from the chilly gusts. So we did, and we hid away. But we could not stay there for ever, and after thirty days our provisions ran out. So we returned to our boat which had frozen to the ice, and dug it out. Boarding and spreading out the canvas sails, we found the boat sailed across the ice as easily as travelling across water. For five days we endured both cold and hunger, until the weather grew milder, the ice broke up, and at the sea turned to water once more.

After sailing for forty miles, we reached a desert island where we were able to replenish our water supplies, and were able to kill two wild bulls, that had horns not on their heads but under their eyes.

Further on the sea turned to milk, and within this strange sea we spied a white island full of grapevines. The island was made of cheese and was some three miles in circumference, while the grapes yielded not wine but milk.

In the middle of the island was a temple, built in honour of Galatea the Nereid. We stayed on the island for five days, using it as our bread and meat, and using the grapes to quench our thirst.

Returning to our boat and departing, the sea slowly changed over three days from milk back to water. Two days later, as we sailed the blue sea, we saw men running across the water's surface. They were like other men in every way, but for their feet which were made of cork. Some bounded over the waves to see us, and greeted us in Greek. They were friendly, and talked to us at length, telling us they were on their way to their capital city, which was also called Cork. For some time they jogged alongside our boat, until they had to turn off, but not before wishing us good luck.

A number of islands came into sight, one of which was made entirely of cork, and there we watched the Cork-Men step ashore. The other islands, five in total, were some way off. Soon we noticed many small fires blazing upon them. The nearest was low-lying and rather flat. As we neared, we could smell a sweet fragrance wafting through the air. The aroma was a mixture of many blooms: roses, violets, lilies and more.

There were woods filled with songbirds, and we could hear pleasant music. It seemed, from what we could hear, that there was a party with people singing and playing instruments. It was so pleasantly intoxicating that we anchored our boat in one of the island's many harbours and went ashore, leaving Scintharus and two sailors aboard.

Advancing through the woodland, we came across some guards who bound us with rose-wreaths and escorted us further inland. As we walked, the guards told us that we were being taken to their leader and that we would have to await our trial. We were fourth in line to face the ruler's judgement, and as we awaited our turn we watched the three preceding trials.

The first case involved Ajax, son of Telamon, who was accused of having turned mad. The judgement was given and Ajax was finally put in the care of Hippocrates, the physician, until he had recovered his wits.

The second trial was to decide if Helen should live with Theseus or Menelaus. After much argument, it was decided that she should live with Menelaus, as he has suffered much to be with her, and Theseus already had a number of wives.

The third case was to determine whether Alexander the Great, outranked Hannibal, and in the end it was decided that this was indeed so.

When we were put on trial we were asked how we had come to the Island of the Blessed while still alive. Only dead heroes were allowed here. We told them of our entire adventure, and then the ruler consulted some of those who were close to him, before pronouncing his verdict. We were told that as we were still alive, they could not try us, and that we were to return there after death for our trial.

For seven months they let us stay with them, before we were taken to a great city of gold and emerald. The gates, seven in all, were of cinnamon, and the ground was pure ivory, while around the city was a river of myrrh.

Within, the residents had no visible form. They bathed in hot dew, heated by burning cinnamon, and wore clothes made of fine, purple spider-webs. We knew of their existence, by their clothes and by the fact that they moved and talked. They were souls, and reminded me of upright shadows, though completely invisible rather than black.

No one there grew old, and similarly the island perpetually hovered around dawn, or perhaps dusk, in permanent gloom. There was also only one continuous season, that of spring, and everywhere was in constant bloom. The fruit trees yielded fruit thirteen times each year, while the grape vines produced grapes once a month. Within the city, there were three hundred and sixty-five water springs, and other springs of honey and of myrrh, and there were also seven milk rivers, and eight wine rivers.

Outside the city was a great table, where the city's inhabitants would often gather. Nearby were glass trees that bore not fruit but cups, and the inhabitants were attended by the winds. Anyone who put a cup on the table would see it fill at once with wine.

Here they sang and recited poetry, usually the works of Homer, who sometimes joined the table. They were also accompanied in song by choruses of boys and girls, and choruses of birds singing from within the woodland.

As well as the springs already mentioned, two others ran close to the table, one filled with laughter and the other with enjoyment. Everyone at the table drank from these as soon as they arrived and so enjoyed themselves and laughed heartily throughout their meal.

While I was there I also met many demigods and legendary heroes. Present were both Cyruses, the Scythian Anacharsis, the divine being Zamolxis, and

Numa Pompilius, the successor of Romulus. In addition, there were Lycurgus of Sparta, Phocion, Tellus of Athens, and, but for Periander of Corinth, all the wise men. I also saw Socrates debating with Nestor and Palamedes. While close to them were Hyacinth of Sparta, Narcissus of Thespiae, Hylas and a host of other great figures.

Socrates seemed to favour Hyacinth above all others, for Hyacinth was someone he happily disagreed with more than anyone else. The wise king of this island, and Judge of the Dead, Rhadamanthus was constantly irritated by Socrates and his self-righteous ways, and Rhadamanthus repeated his threats to banish Socrates from the island unless he became less serious and more jolly.

Plato, the famous student of Socrates, was not there, and it was said that he was living in an imaginary city, that was answerable to the laws and constitution that he himself had written.

Aristippus, Epicurus and their many followers, were held in high regard by many of the heroes, because of their amiable natures. Aesop the great teller of fables was there also, in the role of a jester.

Diogenes the famous Cynic, was there too, but he was a changed man. Instead of criticising everyone and everything, he married Lais the courtesan, and spent most of his time dancing or carrying out silly pranks.

None of the Stoics were there. It was said that they were still journeying up the steep path of virtue. The Academicians had been invited to come to the Island of the Blessed, but they could not cease their debating and take any practical steps. Indeed, one of the topics they debated was the very existence of the island. I imagine too that they feared Rhadamanthus would pass an unfavourable judgement upon them. It was said that some Academicians, had set off for the island, but being unable to agree on just about anything, they only made it half-way before turning back.

The islanders' attitude towards relationships is very open, and they will do any manner of things in public that most would rather keep indoors. Socrates claimed that he had never had relationships with young ladies, but on this matter he was found by everyone to be guilty of perjury. All the men shared their wives with one another, and no one was jealous of other people's relationships.

After a few days, I met Homer, and decided to ask him about his past.

"It's often been debated which part of the world you come from," I said. "Some say you are from Ithica, some say you are from Smyrna, and others say you are from Chios. Could you answer that question once and for all?"

"I am from Babylon," he replied. "My name was Tigranes, but when I was captured by the Greeks and held hostage – or as a Greek like you might also say *homeros* – I changed my name.

"Why did you begin the Iliad with Achilles being in such a state of anger?"

"It just came into my mind that way. The idea wasn't taken from anyone or anywhere else."

"Which of your two great works did you write

first?"

"You mean the Iliad or the Odyssey?"

I nodded. "Most scholars seem to think you wrote the Odyssey first."

"Then they are wrong."

One question I wanted answered was whether or not, as legend had it, he was blind. But I did not have to ask, for it was clear enough that he could see.

I met with Homer many times, and he was happy to answer my many questions. I even broached the delicate matter of when Thersites had accused him of libel. It is true that Thersites had been ridiculed in the Iliad, but with Odysseus as his lawyer, Homer eventually won the case.

While I was there, the mathematician and philosopher, Pythagoras arrived. During his life, his soul had lived in seven bodies and had now ended its migration. The right hand side of his body was made entirely of gold, and after some discussion it was eventually agreed that he could join the Island of the Blessed.

Empedocles came too, his body burned after he perished in Mount Etna, but unlike Pythagoras, and despite his many protests, he was not allowed to stay.

One of the highlights of my stay were the Games of the Dead, with Achilles and Theseus acting as referees. The first competition was wrestling, and Caranus, descendant of Hercules, defeated Odysseus in the final. In the boxing, the final was a draw between Areius and Epeius. I do not remember who won the sprint, but in poetry Hesiod won, even though Homer's writings were far better. Each person who won was awarded a crown adorned with peacock feathers.

To this point, my stay had been a happy one, but it was not to last. Not long after the games, we heard that those who had been imprisoned on the Island of the Wicked had managed to overcome their guards and had set sail for the Island of the Blessed.

Those who had escaped included the tyrant Phalaris of Acragas, Busiris the Egyptian, Diomedes of Thrace, the robber Sciron and the bandit Sinis.

Rhadamanthus gathered together all the heroes on the shore, led by Theseus, Achilles, and Ajax, who had now recovered his wits.

The battle was not long and the heroes soon overcame the invaders. Achilles contributed the greatest amount to their success, but Socrates too exceeded himself, putting up a far better fight than when he had fought at Delium. Even when four of the enemy charged at him, he stood firm. In return for his bravery, Socrates was given a park of his own. Here he was able to gather people around him and engage in debate. These grounds he named the Academy of the Dead.

The defeated army of wicked men were clasped in irons and sent back to their island, where they were to be punished more severely than before. Homer wrote a poem celebrating the victory, and when I later left the island he gave me a copy of the poem which I unfortunately lost. It was also by no means the end of the islanders' troubles.

Cinyras, the son of Scintharus, and an able member of our crew, was a tall, handsome youth who had fallen in love with Menelaus's wife, Helen. It seemed that her romantic feelings for him were even stronger. They often winked and smiled at one another at the table, and they would often go for walks together in the wood.

One day Cinyras and Helen desired to make love, and decided it would be best if they first went to another island. Few people knew of this plan, namely three of my crew who were needed to escort them. Cinyras and Helen feared that Cinyras's father, Scintharus, might find out, for they knew that he was against them having any sort of relationship.

It was late at night when they set off, and most people, including myself, were fast asleep. Helen's husband, Menelaus woke up and upon seeing that his wife was not at his side, caused a great commotion and took his brother with him to see King Rhadamanthus.

When day broke, some lookouts spotted a ship near the horizon, and when the news was passed to King Rhadamanthus, he put fifty men aboard a ship carved from a single log and ordered them to chase down the distant ship.

At noon, just as Helen and Cinyras were entering into the milky waters, on their way to the Island of Cheese, they were caught and escorted home. Helen wept and locked herself in her room filled with shame, while Cinyras and the three other crewmen who had helped him were banished to the Island of the Wicked.

Tainted by association, and for not keeping my men under my control, I, along with the rest of my crew were to spend only one more day on the island before having to leave.

To my shame, I began to cry and weep. I did not want to leave this wondrous place. Many of those that I had befriended tried to cheer me up and reassure me. They told me I would return there again one day, and that my seat was already prepared, and situated close to the best people.

I turned to Rhadamanthus and asked him what my future held.

"You will have a good many adventures before you return to your native land."

"And when will I return to my home?"

But Rhadamanthus did not answer, instead he pointed out to sea, where an island was emitting many plumes of smoke. "That," he said, "is the Island of the Wicked. Nearby I'm sure you can see another four islands, and there in the distance you should be able to see another island."

I nodded.

"That," said Rhadamanthus, "is the Island of Dreams. Further still, and some way out of sight, is the island of Ogygia. When you have sailed past all these islands, you will come to a great continent opposite the one you inhabit."

He picked a mallow root and handed it to me.

"When you are faced with any great danger, pray to this root," he said. "When you reach the great continent, do not eat lupines, do not stoke fires with the blade of your sword, and never make love to anyone over the age of eighteen. Heed these words and you will one day return to this island."

On the day that my crew and I were due to leave, and we walked down to the harbour, I saw that Homer had carved a couplet, dedicated to me, on a slab of polished beryl:

Lucian

Mistrusted at first, but now departs,
Forever remembered in all our hearts.

My crew and I readied ourselves to set sail. Odysseus, without the knowledge of his wife, Penelope, handed me a letter and asked me to take it to Calypso on the Island of Ogygia. Rhadamanthus sent Nauplius, son of Poseidon, to escort us for the first few leagues, so that none of the islanders would suspect us of any untoward motives.

After a few hours of sailing, the fresh breeze that filled my lungs with excitement was soon replaced by a most awful stench. I could smell burning sulphur and asphalt and pitch, and the scent of burning human flesh. The air became foggy with terrible smoke, and as we sailed half-blind we began to hear the wails and cries of men.

We saw a natural harbour and moored our ship. Had we continued, barely able to see more than a few feet ahead, we might well have smashed into rocks. Setting foot on the island, there didn't appear to be any animals or even plants, there was bare rock everywhere.

Only after we had climbed a sheer cliff, did we see any plants, all big and ugly and full of thorns. As we hacked our way through, we saw that sword blades and metal traps protruded from the ground. During our trek, we came across three rivers; one of mud, one of blood and another of lava. The river of lava was impossible to cross. Peering into it, we could make out many fish swimming under the surface, some resembled coals, and others resembled flaming torches.

Walking alongside the fiery river, we came upon Timon of Athens. He was suspicious at first, but upon seeing Nauplius, he said that he would guide us. We were escorted to a part of the island where people, including kings, were being tormented with flames, as punishment for previous misdeeds. Those who endured the worst punishment, and whose voices we had earlier heard crying out, were those people who had told lies all their life, and written untrue histories. Among them I recognized Ctesias of Cnidos, and Heroditus. I was happy that such people were the ones who were punished, for I have never knowingly told a lie.

It was a horrific sight, and I could hardly endure the terrible screams, so we returned to the ship. Fortunately a change of wind had blown away the horrible fog, and after saying goodbye to Nauplius, we sailed away.

A few hours passed before the next island, the Island of Dreams, came into sight. It was somewhat vague in shape and position. As we approached, it would sometimes be nearer and sometimes further away, but before we gave up hope of ever reaching it, we suddenly found ourselves in a harbour, near some ivory gates.

Disembarking, we walked through the gates, then

between two springs and a river, and into the city mentioned only by Homer. Here there were trees that were not really trees at all, but tall poppies and mandragoras. Within them were bats, the only winged creatures to inhabit the island.

The wall that surrounded the city was rainbow-coloured, and there were not two city gates, as Homer says, but four. Two of these gates, one of iron and the other earthenware, were where nightmares exited, while the other two, including the one we passed through, faced the sea.

There was a temple in the city, to the right of the gate we entered, dedicated to the worship of the night, and to the left of the entrance was a palace where resides Sleep. There were two other temples in the heart of the town, one of falsehood and one of truth. It was said that Antiphon, the interpreter of dreams, also lived in this city.

Dreams made up the general population. Some dreams were tall and handsome, while others were squat and ugly. Some, it seemed to me were rich, while others resembled beggars.

We recognized many dreams, and many of them came to us and greeted us like old friends. They took us to their homes, put us to sleep, and entertained us as we slumbered. We stayed for a month, and during that time, one dream took me with him back to my homeland for one evening where I caught sight of my friends and family.

A great boom of thunder woke us all up, and we wondered if anything we had witnessed had really happened, and we once more set out to sea.

After three days we reached the island of Ogygia, and here I opened Odysseus's letter and read it:

Greetings dear Calypso,

I have not had the opportunity to tell you what happened to me after I left you, but now is my first chance. After I built the raft and left your island, I was shipwrecked. With Leucothea's help, I was able to journey home. When I arrived, I saw that my wife had many suitors, all of whom were living off her goodwill. I killed every one of them, but later on I was killed by Telegonus, my son by Circe. Now I live on the Island of the Blessed. I am sorry for having left you and your offer of immortality. If I ever get the chance, dear Calypso, I will leave this island and join you, and we might spend eternity together.

The letter also asked that Calypso entertain us, and we found her in a cave, close to the sea, much as Homer had described.

When Calypso read the letter, she wept. Eventually she dispelled her tears, and gave us a great feast. As we ate, she asked about Odysseus and about Penelope, and we gave her the answers that we thought she might wish to hear.

The next morning we left the island, only to be caught up in a storm that lasted two days. No sooner had the storm subsided however, than we were attacked by pirates. They sailed boats made of giant, hollowed-out melons, with reeds for masts and giant leaves for sails. As they attacked they hurled giant seeds at us, which were as hard as stones, and during hand-to-hand combat many of my crew were bludgeoned with them.

After an hour of deadlock, we saw men sailing ships made of giant nutshells. The melon-pirates left us as quickly as they had attacked and went off instead to fight the nut-people. We fled, knowing no good would come to us if we loitered, and I looked back now and again to see those on-board the nut-boats clearly had the upper hand and would eventually be victorious.

We attended to the wounded, and from that point kept a more vigilant lookout, lest we find ourselves caught off guard once more.

Our vigilance paid off, for as we passed a desert island, we saw twenty men riding dolphins as though they were horses. The dolphins leapt and dived and neighed, and the men, who we soon discovered were also pirates, never lost their balance. When they were only yards away, they bombarded us with dry cuttle-fish and crabs' eyes. We threw spears and arrows back at them, and they were soon beaten, and they fled back to their island where they tended to the wounded.

Our next encounter took place at around midnight when, in the darkness, we ran aground, and found we had become stranded on a giant bird's nest, made not of twigs but of trees. The nest was floating and indeed moving, pulled by the currents, and in the middle of the nest a giant bird was sitting on her eggs. She began to cry out and beat her wings, and the wind they created almost sunk our ship. She flew up and out of sight, and while she was gone, we cut open some of the eggs with our axes. Inside were featherless chicks, larger than twenty vultures, and we took one of them back to the ship. After moving some tree branches to free our ship, we were able to set sail.

We had travelled ten leagues or so, when the chick we had captured began to suddenly sprout feathers. What was even more amazing was that Scintharus, who was completely bald, now had a thick head of hair. More astounding still was the mast which, suddenly grew branches, then leaves and figs.

We prayed to the gods, for we were very disturbed by these strange and sudden occurrences. Ahead, we saw a forest of pine trees and cypresses, and indeed this forest seemed to run the length of the horizon in front of us. But all was not as it seemed. As we came closer, we saw that this was not a densely wooded island, but rootless trees, upright and floating.

As we could not go round, or thought it would take too long to do so, we made a rope, climbed the trees and pulled the ship up. The trees were so closely packed that they easily held us and our vessel. We clambered aboard, spread our canvas and, with a good wind behind us, we sailed across the treetops as easily as crossing the ocean.

Reaching the other side of the strange wood, we let the boat down once more, and continued our journey through clear waters.

Our next obstacle was something quite different; the ocean had a great crack running the length of it, as though made by some great earthquake. We were blown right to the edge, where I looked down to see a sheer drop of at least a thousand furlongs. The water did not tumble down however, instead it remained where it was. To our right, at no great distance, was a river, bridging the crack. We rowed away from the edge, and with some effort we crossed the watery bridge.

The sea on the other side was quite calm, and we reached a small island where we saw people who resembled the great Minotaur. They were a savage race. We were out of food and water, and having taken water from a river, we went in search of food. But we had not gone far when we heard a bellow. At first we thought we had come across cattle, but then we were attacked by these bull-men. Three of my crew were captured and the rest of us were chased back to our ship. We did not have to talk for long before agreeing to go back and avenge our friends. We armed ourselves, and went back, attacking the bull-men as they feasted on our companions.

We killed fifty of them and took two back to our ship as prisoners. We still had no food and some of the hungry crew suggested we eat our enemy. But I had other ideas, and we clasped the bull-men in irons and waited until a delegation of bull-men approached us. In return for the two captives we were given cheeses, fish, onions, and four does, each of which had only three legs – two hind legs and fused forelegs.

We did not wait any more time than necessary before once more setting out to sea. We soon saw fish and birds and other signs that we were approaching land, and travelling a little further we saw beings that were both sailors and ships. They lay on their backs, on the water, and they tied sails to a certain part of their anatomy which they used as masts. Others, sat on corks and were pulled along by dolphins. These strange people neither attacked nor fled from us, but wondered at our boat with quizzical looks.

As dusk came, we anchored our ship by a small island, inhabited by women, or so we thought. They were all young and wore tunics that swept the ground, and to our surprise they all spoke perfect Greek. They also made us feel most welcome, and embraced every one of us.

Each woman escorted one man back to their home and made him her guest. I was invited back by a most beautiful young woman, but I had my misgivings and declined her invitation. As my companions disappeared, I wandered round and saw human bones and skulls. I was tempted to shout aloud and call my crew back, but instead I grabbed my mallow, and prayed to it.

I returned to the spot where I had declined the young woman's invitation and saw that she was still there, waiting. I let her escort me back to her home, and it was as we entered that I glimpsed not her feet, but hooves. Startled I made a few more surreptitious glances and saw that her legs were those of an ass.

I drew my sword, caught her and held the blade against her neck. I asked her who she was and what her people intended to do with my men.

"We are women of the sea," she said. "When we have intoxicated your men, we will kill them and eat them."

I tied her up and ran outside where I called for my companions. I told them the story and showed them the bones, but when I took them to the woman I had tied up, she had turned to a pool of water. I took my sword and plunged it into the water, which quickly turned crimson.

We fled to the boat and sailed away in the darkness. By dawn, we saw land on the horizon, and none of us doubted that this was the continent that Rhadamanthus had told us about; the continent on the other side of the world. We made an offering to the gods, and discussed whether or not our expedition should end here. Some argued that we had been fortunate enough to get this far, and that now was the time to go home. Others said we should explore the continent's interior.

But the elements made the decision for us – a storm like none we had encountered before whipped up in a matter of minutes and our ship was thrown towards the land and smashed upon rocks. We all swam towards the beach, and to an uncertain future.

So now I have told you of our trip to the Moon, our adventure inside the great whale, our time with the heroes, and the host of strange islands we visited, but what happened in this other world will be revealed to you in the next book.

Icaro-Menippus

Lucian of Samosata

Introduction

Lucian of Samosata (125–c.180) was a Greek satirist of Syrian or Assyrian extraction, and is perhaps best-known for his story *True History*. *Icaro-Menippus* is a satirical play with Greek philosophers being the focus of Lucian's ridicule. The play contains only two characters: Menippus, and an unnamed friend. Mennipus tells his companion how he used bird wings to fly into space, visiting the Moon and the Greek gods during his travels. Whether or not Mennipus's story is true is left for the audience to decide.

Characters in the Play

Menippus
An Unnamed Friend

Icaro-Menippus

Lucian of Samosata

[A friend overhears Menippus talking to himself, and approaches him.]

MENIPPUS (muttering): Now let me think. The distance from the Earth to the Moon is around three hundred and forty miles. And then to the Sun, that must be another fifteen hundred miles. And from there to Heaven and to Jupiter's palace, well, by my reckoning that's about the distance a swift eagle might cover in a day.

FRIEND: What are you whispering, Menippus? I've been following you these last few minutes, listening as you talk to yourself in a most abstracted manner, about the Moon and the stars and the Sun, and the distances between them.

MENNIPUS: Don't be too amazed if my words sound strange and startling. I am simply calculating the distance I travelled on my latest journey.

FRIEND: I see. You've been using the night sky to help you find your bearings, just as the Phoenicians do.

MENIPPUS: You are wrong my friend. I haven't used the Moon and the Heavens to guide me – I have just returned from travelling among the stars themselves.

FRIEND: You mean you have had a dream – and a long dream at that if you travelled such vast distances.

MENIPPUS: It was no dream. I have just returned from Jupiter!

FRIEND: What? You mean you have literally descended from the Heavens?

MENIPPUS: That is exactly what happened. I have only just returned from Jupiter, where I heard and saw the strangest things. I see you doubt me, but no matter, it makes my trip even more satisfying when I think it is beyond the belief of others.

FRIEND: How could a man as humble as myself not believe the words of the divine Menippus? How could I doubt the word of someone, who has flown above the clouds, and who Homer might call an 'inhabitant of Heaven'? But tell me how you managed to reach such lofty heights. Where did you find a ladder big enough for you to climb so high – or were you snatched up by a giant eagle, and whisked off into the Heavens?

MENIPPUS: I'm not surprised you see my story as a joke, given all I have said, but my story is no fable, I assure you. I needed no ladder, or an eagle, for I had wings of my own.

FRIEND: Why this is more amazing than the tale of Daedalus and Icarus! Did you turn into a hawk or some other bird when we were not looking?

MENIPPUS: Well, for all your scoffing, you are quite close to the truth. I did copy Daedalus's idea of using wings to fly.

FRIEND: Well if you tried that idea then you're a fool. Did you want the wax that held your feathers in place to melt, so that you might plunge into the sea, and have it named after you just as happened to Icarus? I can imagine it now – The Menippean Sea.

MENIPPUS: I had no such intention. I did not use wax because I didn't want to plunge from the sky like Icarus.

FRIEND: Then what did you use?

MENIPPUS: I caught a powerful eagle and a large vulture, and then I cut off their wings for my own use. If you have the time I will happily tell you, from beginning to end, of my flight into the Heavens.

FRIEND: Please do. I would love to know what happened. I feel like the suspense – suspended by the ears that is – is all too much.

MENIPPUS: Listen then – I would never leave a friend who has been suspended by his ears.

I had thought much about human affairs like wealth and power, law and politics and so on, and I came to the conclusion that such things were trivial and near-worthless, not least compared with the majesty of the universe. I was excited to meditate on things that to me were new and profound: How had the universe come into being? Who had made it? Had there been a beginning – and would there be an end?

But the more I investigated, the more confused I became. I looked up at the stars, seemingly scattered at random across the sky, I looked at the Sun and wondered what it was made of, and I looked at the Moon, which appeared to me to be the most magnificent thing in the sky, and I wondered why on some nights it was full and on others it was not. I puzzled over the descent of rain and hail and snow, and I wanted to know about thunder and lightning. All of these things swirled in my mind and I longed to know their nature.

I thought that to get some answers I would be best off consulting the philosophers. I was sure they could put my mind at rest. So I selected the best of them, judging their wisdom by their complexion, their poses, and the length of their beards. After choosing from these many men with their lofty thoughts and even loftier words, I placed myself in their hands. And after happily taking a tidy some of money, and receiving my guarantee that they would receive yet more money after my training, they began to instruct me.

I had hoped that I would become a man of wisdom, and a great orator on many profound subjects. But far from dispelling my ignorance, they instead managed to confuse me even more, with their talk of atoms and voids, beginnings and ends, matter and form, and goodness knows what else. And worst of all, they couldn't even agree with one another, and each of them expected me to believe him, and subscribe to his beliefs.

FRIEND: How funny that such wise men should disagree so vehemently, holding so many opinions on the same things.

MENIPPUS: You'll find it funnier still when I tell you about their pretentious drivel. These philosophers, who are no taller than ourselves yet walk about with self-satisfied grandeur, are neither wiser nor sharper-sighted than the rest of us, and yet they go about saying how they can measure the circumference of the Sun, work out the shape and size of stars and even walk upon the Moon. All these lofty claims, from men who could not say how many miles it is from Athens to Megara. They even claim to be able to calculate the distance from the Moon to the Sun, how high the atmosphere is and the depth of the sea. I have seen them scribbling down numbers, and drawing squares and triangles and circles, and then suddenly they cry that they have calculated the volume of Heaven itself.

They happily speak without the slightest self-doubt. They swear that the Sun is a molten mass of liquid fire, that the Moon is inhabited, that the stars drink water, and that the Sun draws vapour from the sea be means of a bucket and rope, before shedding the load across the world.

They disagree with each other on so many points. Some believe that the world had no beginning and can have no end, some say the world, and indeed the universe, had a Creator, and talk as though they know everything about Him. But they will not say where he came from, nor where he resides, nor how the ideas of time and space could have existed before the universe began.

FRIEND: They really do sound like a bunch of verbal conjurers.

MENIPPUS: I wish I could tell you more about their arguments over ideal and incorporeal substances, and over things finite and infinite. On the latter point there is much disagreement. Some philosophers believe everything has boundaries, others say there are no limits. Some say there is but one world, while others say there are many. There is even one man who claims that war is the father of the universe.

When it comes to divinity they are even more divided. Some say god is a number, while others swear by dogs and geese and trees. Some say there is only one god – an idea I find almost too depressing to contemplate. Others furnish their theories with a liberal sprinkling of gods, giving them tasks to undertake, and also rank them according to divinity. Some assumed the gods were entities that neither had substance nor shape. Others believed they had bodies, like most living creatures. There was disagreement over whether or not gods intervened in human affairs. Some philosophers claimed the gods intervened at regular intervals, while their philosopher-opponents claimed that the gods resided in the background, like men who had retired from civic duty.

Some philosophers went further still and claimed that there were no gods at all. They asserted that the world drifts without any guide or master.

I listened intently to every philosopher and, to begin with at least, I did not dare contradict any of those men with their long words and longer beards. But as they contradicted one another I became confused. Whenever I thought that one of them had a valid point and I began to believe that they had struck upon an unassailable truth, doubts would creep into my mind.

But during my distress, and perhaps as a result of it, I decided that rather than use theory and counter theory to discover truths about the universe, why not travel there and see the answer for myself? So it was that I decided to escape these men of words, and to fashion myself some wings and fly to the Heavens. Indeed I was heartened when picking up a copy of Aesop's Fables, and read that beetles, eagles and even camels had succeeded in reaching the Heavens.

Obviously I could not sprout wings of my own, so I decided to use those of an eagle and a vulture – wings that were powerful enough to lift a man from the ground, of course. I caught an eagle, and a vulture, and I amputated the eagle's right wing and the vulture's left wing. I fastened them to my arms with loops of material, and near the wing tips were two more loops for my hands to hold.

Then I was ready to begin my experiments. To begin with I simply jumped up and down and flapped my wings. Then I began to imitate geese, the way they spread out their wings and run across the ground and take off. To begin with I simply skimmed the ground, but then I became bold and ventured to the top of the Acropolis. Steeling myself, I leapt, and found myself not falling but flying downwards into the theatre. Landing safely, I found almost all my fear had disappeared. Starting from Hymettus I flew to Geranea. From there I flew on to the top of the tower at Corinth, and then I travelled over Pholoe, and then from Erymanthus to Taygetus.

But this was merely a chicken's flight compared with my ultimate aim. Now my training was complete, and my arms were powerfully strong. I took provisions with me and soared up to the top of Mount Olympus.

The Heavens were above me and the world far below me, and from here I soared further into the sky. Looking down as I flew made me feel quite giddy at first, but this soon wore off. I looked ahead and set my course for the Moon.

I had not planned to land on the Moon, and soon even the clouds were far behind me, but by this point I was tiring, especially in the vulture wing. So as soon as I reached the Moon I decided to land.

I sat myself down and, with my bird's-eye view, I looked back upon the Earth. So, like Homer's Jupiter, I was able to survey the Thracian horsemen, the Mycians, and the people of India, Persia and Greece. All of whom I observed with great delight.

FRIEND: Tell me everything you can about your travels, and don't omit a single detail. Recount, if you would, all you saw and heard. I would love to know the shape of the Earth, and how it appeared to someone who stood upon the Moon, observing it.

MENIPPUS: I will tell you all you desire. But first you will have to travel, in your imagination, to the Moon, with my words for guidance. Then turn to face the Earth. When I was there and looked down upon the Earth, it appeared to me to be far smaller than the Moon. At first I could not make out the great mountains of the Earth, or the vast seas, until I spotted the colossus of Rhodes, and the tower of Pharus. Indeed without spotting these great monuments, it would have been impossible to recognise our world.

But my eyes soon began to focus and make sense of what they saw, and when the light from the Sun grew a little stronger and began to glint off the ocean waves, I was able to make out a great deal. I could see nations and cities and the whole of the human race. I saw men waging war, ploughing fields and sailing the seas, and I saw women, animals and, in short, I beheld every creature that roamed upon the Earth.

FRIEND: That really is a most unconvincing and contradictory story Menippus. You said that the Earth was tiny in size, far smaller than the Moon. You said that had it not been for the colossus of Rhodes you wouldn't have seen it at all. Then, you contradict yourself, and talk of being able to make out men and women and animals. Had I let you talk further, no doubt you would have told me how you observed, from that great distance, a nest of fleas.

MENIPPUS: Of course – thank you for reminding me! I forgot to mention that at first I had been able to make out the Earth but as it was so far away, I could not pick out any particular details on its surface. I was horribly frustrated by my situation and felt I might burst into tears, but before I was swallowed whole by misery who should turn up but the physicist Empedocles. He looked as black as coal, covered in ashes, and scorched as though he'd just stepped out of an oven. I must admit to having been terrified upon seeing this strange figure, thinking he was some sort of Moon Creature.

"Do not be afraid," he reassured me. "I am no demon, but a man like yourself. Friend, I am Empedocles, the physicist. You may know the tale of how I climbed to the summit Mount Etna, and threw myself into its volcanic crater. But I did not die, instead the billowing smoke lifted me high into the Heavens and deposited me here. Now I live on the Moon, feeding on dew, and spending most of my days philosophizing. I can see you are distressed, and I am here to help you fulfil your wish to see everything on Earth."

"Thank you Empedocles," I said. "When I return to Greece, I will burn offerings to you, and will send them up my chimney once every month."

"There is no need," said Empedocles. "I am not helping you so that I might be rewarded. I was saddened to see your distress, so decided to help. Now what do you think might help you see in great detail all that goes on, amongst the humans of Earth?"

"I have no idea," I said. "It all seems so hazy. It is as though my eyes are straining to see through mist, and unless you can get rid of this blurred vision I doubt I'll be able to see anything."

"You don't need me to improve your sight," said Empedocles. "You have brought the necessary piece of equipment with you."

"Really?" I said, rather startled.

"Of course," he replied. "It is your eagle's wing, which you wear on your right arm."

"But how does that help?" I asked. "What has an eagle's wing to do with improving my eyesight?"

"A lot," he replied. "As you may know, the eagle has the best eyesight of any living creature. This bird is the only one that can stare at the Sun without blinking."

"So I have heard," I said. "But I do not have the eyes of an eagle. Perhaps I should have not only taken the eagle's wing, but his eyes also and replaced mine with them."

"You may still acquire one eagle eye," said Empedocles.

I looked at him, puzzled.

He continued: "You must beat your eagle wing up and down, while keeping the vulture wing absolutely still. As you do this, your right eye will gain in strength, until you are able to see all you wish to on the world below. Your left eye however, being on the side of the vulture wing will always remain inferior, and there is nothing that can be done about this."

"I am happy enough to have such brilliance of vision in just one eye," I said. "I do not need it in both. Indeed I have seen carpenters and artists occasionally making use of just one eye rather than two, and if it is good enough for them, it is good enough for me."

I began at once to flap my eagle wing and, knowing his work was done, Empedocles turned into smoke, then faded and disappeared.

FRIEND: That really is astounding.

MENIPPUS: Indeed, and there were still more amazing things to come. So I continued to beat my wing, and as I did so the mist lifted from before my eyes and I was able to see the world with the sharpness of an eagle.

Looking down on the Earth, I could see cities and men and all that took place. Strangely, I was able to see not only what took place in the open but what happened inside people's homes. I saw Lysimachus plotting to execute his eldest son, Agathocles; Antiochus conspiring with his mother-in-law; Alexander the Thessalian being killed by his wife; Attalus being poisoned by his son; Arsaces murdering his mistress; the eunuch Arbaces killing Arsaces; guards dragging Spatinus the Mede from the banquet by his heels and then struck over the head with a golden cup.

In the palaces of Scythia and Lybia and Thrace I saw nothing but murder, adultery, treason, robbery, conspiracies, suspicion and people betrayed by their so-called friends. So this was the life lead by royalty and nobility, but in the private houses there was still more to see. I saw Hermodorus the Epicurean perjuring himself for a thousand dracmas; Agathocles the Stoic trying to extract fees from one of his pupils;

The orator, Clinias, stealing a phial from the temple of Asclepius, and I saw Herophilus the Cynic visiting a brothel.

And then there was the rest of the population, robbers, burglars, fraudsters and others who put on a fine spectacle for me.

FRIEND: What entertainment! I wish I'd been there with you to witness it all. But please, tell me more.

MENIPPUS: I'm afraid I saw too much to recount to you here. Indeed so much went on even my eagle eye could not take it all in. There were feasts and marriages, arguments and burials. The Getae were at war, there were Scythians travelling in their caravans, the Egyptians were ploughing their fields, the Cilicians were robbing and plundering, the Phoenicians were flogging their wares, the Spartans were flogging one another, and the Athenians – a litigious lot – were forever taking one another to court.

All this was happening simultaneously, you must understand, and it was all rather confusing. It was as though a choir had been told not to sing harmoniously, but to sing their own songs, and to ensure that they were heard above the rest. I'm sure you can imagine what a deafening cacophony it would be.

FRIEND: It must have been the most ridiculous and confusing sight.

MENIPPUS: Alas, it was. All those Earthly performers putting on their confused spectacle, and showing that the life of man is just that – a confused spectacle. Their voices are discordant, their movements are not synchronous, the set is not agreed upon, and so it goes on, until the director dismisses every one of them from the stage, telling them they are no longer wanted. Then they are all silent, and no longer shout over one another in this cacophonous chorus. This theatre is wide and diverse, where there is plenty to ridicule and laugh about.

Those who entertained me the most however, were those who argued and fought over the boundaries of their tiny territories, or thought themselves high and mighty because they worked on the plains of Sicyon, or those who prided themselves on holding the border between Marathon and Oenoe, or those who fancied themselves because they owned a thousand acres in Acharnae.

As I gazed down at Greece, it appeared so small that it might have fitted in the palm of my hand. And Athens, well, it was truly minute. I realized that these pompous men were priding themselves over the tiniest pieces of land. The greatest landowner of them all appeared to be lord of nothing more than an atom.

I glanced towards the Peloponnese, and towards Cynuria, where I saw that for the tiniest fragment of land, no bigger than a lentil, an astonishing number of Spartans and Argives were slaughtered.

I also saw a man who thought far too much of himself because he owned eight gold rings and four gold cups – I could help but laugh at the fellow! Even Pangaeus, with all its mines, seemed no larger than a grain of millet.

FRIEND: What a sight that must have been. I would dearly love to know how large the towns and their residents seemed to you.

MENIPPUS: I'm sure you've seen ants scurrying about, sometimes alone and sometimes in great numbers busying themselves in their own little city. One might be rolling something, another pushing a bean or a grain of wheat. Even on their tiny scale, I have no doubt that they have their own architects, politicians, musicians, philosophers and the like. And when I looked down, to see men and their cities, they reminded me of ants and their ant-hills. If you think my comparison too unfair, then you would do well to recollect the Thessalian tales, and you will find that the Myrmidons – ants that had turned into men – were the most war-like of people.

When I had had my fill of observing all of humanity on this tiny planet, and meditating on the insignificance of human affairs, I turned my back, started to jog and then run, and as I pick up speed my feet left the ground. But before I could begin my flight towards the land of the Gods, the Moon in her soft, feminine voice cried out to me:

"Menippus!"

I landed back on the ground.

"Menippus," she said again, "please take with you something of mine to Jupiter. If you do, I promise that you shall prosper from your journey."

"I would gladly carry something for you," I replied. "So long as I am strong enough to take it with me."

"It weighs nothing at all," said the Moon. "It is a

message that I wish you to take; a petition addressed to Jupiter himself. I have become so very tired by the philosophers of your world – I am almost at my wit's end. They seem to have nothing better to do than talk about me, as though I have no feelings. Just how big am I? they ask. Who am I? Why am I sometimes full, sometimes half-full and sometimes vanish altogether? Am I merely a mirror hanging over the sea? Am I inhabited? I'm so tired of their endless speculations and conjectures. And just when I thought they couldn't get any worse, they began to suggest the light that I radiate is not my own, but stolen from my own brother, the Sun. I can't believe they would suggest such a thing, and try to turn us against one another. It was bad enough when they said he was a red-hot stone, but now they've really gone too far.

"These philosophers, with their long beards and grave countenances, who act so rationally during the day, would be surprised to know that I see exactly what they get up to at night. But I say nothing of their adultery or thieving or any other shameful pursuit. I have never even considered making these facts known to the wider public, instead, when I see their vile ways, I wrap myself in a thick cloud. I don't want to watch these dirty old creatures and their disgusting habits.

"But these fiends, guilty of every vice, go on abusing me and sullying my reputation. It has upset me so greatly, that I have often considered flying away so that I might never see or hear another philosopher again.

"Please, tell Jupiter all that I have said, and that if nothing is done I will leave, never to return. I want him to destroy all physicists, silence the logicians and burn the Academy down, so that I might finally have the rest which these so-called wise men perpetually deny me."

"I will pass your message on," I promised, and I flew into the air, and away from the Moon, until she was quite small, and the Earth was hidden behind her.

With the Sun on my right hand side, I flew for three days through the stars, where no man had travelled before, until I finally reached my destination – the entrance to Heaven. My first thought was to fly straight in. The eagle was well known to Jupiter, and now being half an eagle, I thought I might enter without raising any suspicion. But it then occurred to me that my vulture wing might betray me. So instead I walked up to the door and knocked.

Mercury answered the door, and after I had told him my name, he went to inform Jupiter. Upon Mercury's return, he asked me to step in, and I did so, trembling with apprehension.

I soon saw, right in front of me, the gods, sitting together, looking at me with suspicion and more than a little fear. I imagined that they were worried that I might be the first of an army of winged mortals on their way to the land of the gods.

Jupiter looked straight at me with a Titanic and penetrating stare.

"Who are you?" he boomed. "From where have you come? From whom are you descended?"

Such was the thunder of his voice, I thought I might die from fright. But I somehow remained standing, though at first I was unable to speak, such was my condition. I was able to compose myself, and then I recounted my whole tale: how I had been fascinated by the Heavens and wanted to know all about them; how I had visited the philosophers, only to hear them contradict one another and ultimately leave me none the wiser; how I had decided to seek the answers for myself and made wings and flown from Earth to Heaven.

I told him too of my visit to the Moon, and told him of her woes, just as she had asked. When Jupiter was told this, his hard expression softened, and then he gave me a large smile.

"Who are Otus and Ephialtes in comparison with Menippus?" said Jupiter. "This mortal man who stands before us has flown up to Heaven. Mennipus, you may stay here the evening as our guest, and tomorrow we will discuss matters of business, and then you may return to Earth."

When he had finished speaking, he stood up and, beckoning me, took me on a journey to a part of Heaven where people's prayers and petitions could be heard. As we walked he asked me a great many questions: How much wheat is there presently in Greece? Had the previous winter been a harsh one? Did our vegetables need more rain? Were any of Phidias's family still alive? Why had Athenians stopped making their sacrifices to the gods? Were they going to continue building the Olympian temple again? Had the robbers that had plundered the temple at Dodona been caught?

I was fortunate to be able to answer all his questions, to his apparent satisfaction, and then he asked another:

"Pray tell me, Menippus – what do people really think about me?"

"Why," I replied, "they think of you just as they should – they look upon the king of gods with the greatest respect and veneration."

"Come now," said Jupiter, "I know that's not true. But long ago I was well respected, when I healed the sick, answered their prayers, and did almost everything that was asked of me.

"Back then Dodona and Pisa were two of the finest places on Earth, and I was unable to see them through all the smoke that came from their sacrifices. Now though it's all changed: Apollo has set up his oracle at Delphi; Aesculapius practices as a healer at Pergamus; temples have been erected to Bendis at Thrace, to Anubis in Egypt, and to Diana at Ephesus. Now people flock to these places instead, and devote themselves to other gods. If they make some sacrificial offering to me every few years at Mount Olympus, people think they're being more than generous.

"It really does seem as though I'm surplus to requirements these days. Now people are about as interested in my altars as they are in Plato's laws, or even Chrysippus's syllogisms."

So we walked on, until we reached the part of Heaven where people's prayers and petitions could be heard. Here there was a row of shafts, each with a lid over the top, and next to each one was a gold chair.

Jupiter seated himself, and opened the first lid. I could hear a babble of voices, and I knelt by the side of the hole, trying to discern what was being said. I was able to snatch a few wishes:

"Oh, Jupiter! Make me the ruler of a large and wealthy empire!"

"Dear gods, let my vegetables flourish!"

"Jupiter – please kill my father!"

"Jupiter – let my wife die, so that I might inherit her property!"

"I beg of you – do not let them find out about my treacherous plans against my brother!"

"Let me be victorious in my impending trial."

"Jupiter, let me be crowned at Olympia."

I heard these and more. One wish was from a sailor who desired a north wind, while another sailor prayed for a south wind. I heard one farmer wish for more Sunlight and another wish for rain.

Jupiter listened patiently, and after careful consideration he granted what he considered to be righteous prayers to come up the shaft and into Heaven. Then he blew all those prayers he considered unworthy back down, so that they would not pollute Heaven.

I remember one case where Jupiter was puzzled. Two men asked for contrary wishes to be granted, much like the two who had desired opposing winds, and to make things even more difficult, they had offered Jupiter the same sacrifice as a token. Jupiter did not know who to favour, and he became a brilliant academic, whose mind was able to hold these opposite wishes in perfect equilibrium, just like Pyrrho.

When he had finally dispensed with the prayers, he passed onto the next seat and lifted the lid of another shaft. Here he took on board vows being made and oaths being sworn.

Next he destroyed Hermodorus the Epicurean, who had been found guilty of perjury. On the following seat, Jupiter dealt with auguries, prophets and sooth sayers. After that, he sat by the shaft where the smoke of the sacrificed dead wafted up and into Heaven, and where those sacrificed told Jupiter the names of those who had sacrificed them.

Once he had heard all the names, he gave orders to the elements:

"Let there be rain in Scythia today, thunder and lightning across the North of Africa, and snow in Greece. The North Wind shall blow in Lydia while the South Wind shall rest today. I want a storm to be raised in the Adriatic, and hail to be cast over Cappadocia."

At last his work in this strange place was done and the lids were closed once more. We retired from this part of Heaven and feasted with the other gods. Mercury guided me to me seat, and I found myself in the company of lesser-gods Pan, the Corybantes, Attis, and Sabazius.

I was handed some bread by Ceres, and Baccus poured me plenty of wine. Hercules dished out the meat, Venus gave out myrtle, and Neptune doled out sea food. While my dining companions were occupied in eating or conversation, good-natured Ganymede slipped me a little nectar and ambrosia without anyone noticing. The Gods, as Homer says (and presumably he has gained such knowledge by visiting Heaven as I have) never feast on bread nor wine, but instead eat ambrosia and drink nectar. Their favourite indulgence however is neither of these, for the gods love nothing more than to inhale the fumes that rise up from victims, and smell the blood of those sacrificed on altars.

During the meal we were treated to many fine performances: Apollo played his harp, Silenus danced, and the Muses sang many songs for us, including Pindar's first ode. After we had eaten and had been greatly entertained, we all slept. Or, I should say, the gods all slept, but my mind was too restless, frothing with a myriad of thoughts. How was it, I wondered, that Apollo in his many years had never grown a beard? With the Sun present, how was it that I could see the night sky?

Eventually I was able to slide into a brief slumber, and early in the morning Jupiter arose and woke the rest of us up. He gathered the gods together into an assembly and addressed them:

"I am addressing you this morning," he began. "because of the stranger who came here yesterday and is with us still. I have wanted, for some time, to discuss the matter of the philosophers, and now that the Moon has petitioned us, it is time we did something about this matter. There is a group that has, in recent times, come about; a group of the laziest, most quarrelsome, vain, foolish, greedy, rude, pompous men to have walked upon the Earth. They have split into many groups who each wrap themselves in an impenetrable shroud of words, and call themselves Stoics, Epicureans, Peripatetics, and too many other names to count. They call themselves virtuous, and with their eyebrows and flowing beards they put on a great appearance of morality to hide their immoral behaviour. It is a performance, worthy of any actor who, if you pulled off his mask and robe, would be seen for what he is – a weedy man hired to appear for a few drachmas.

"These philosophers happily go around despising everyone, they spread lies about the gods, and gather together gullible young men and fill their minds with worthless information. These young disciples are told by their masters to scorn riches and pleasures, and to embrace fortitude and temperance. These same masters who, when they are alone, indulge in every form of debauchery. But their worst offence is that they do nothing and help no one. They contribute no good to society, they merely sneer at ordinary folk, continually finding fault in the words and actions of people in their community.

"If someone were to ask a philosopher, 'What useful role do you play in society?' he, if he had the ability to speak fairly and truthfully, would reply, 'It is beneath my dignity to be a farmer or sailor or soldier, or work in trade. But I do have a loud voice and a dirty body, I scrub myself in cold water, and go barefoot all winter and then, like Momus, I find fault with others. If a wealthy man purchases something expensive, I abuse him. If a friend is ill, and needs help and care, I take no notice of them.'

"This then is the kind of man we are dealing with. And of all these philosophers, the Epicureans are the worst. They say the gods take no interest in human affairs, and have no effect on the course of human lives. If these Epicureans spread their beliefs, and people think that we do nothing for them, then they will no longer make sacrifices, and we will starve. As to the Moon's complaints, you heard all this from the stranger yesterday.

"Now you must decide among yourselves what is to be done with these philosophers, both for the benefit of ourselves and the happiness of mankind."

Jupiter had barely finished speaking, when the gods cried out: "Blast them with thunder and lightning! Burn them all! Throw them all the way down to Tartarus, and to the giants!"

Jupiter raised his hand and asked for silence. "Your will shall be done," his voice boomed. "The philosophers shall be destroyed along with their philosophy – but not just yet. As you are all aware, I have declared a truce for the next four months, but when Spring comes, and the truce is over, I shall fire lightning bolts at them and give them the punishment they deserve."

Then, as soon as the counsel began to break up, my wings were removed, and I was carried by Mercury back down to Earth.

So now my friend you have heard my story, and know all about Heaven. But I really must be off to the Poecile, and tell my good news to the philosophers.

Urashima Taro

Introduction

Urashima Taro is the earliest known time-travel tale. This story was written by an unknown Japanese author and dates from around the eighth century. It tells of a fisherman who saves a turtle from being tormented by children, and who is rewarded with a trip beneath the sea to the palace of a dragon god. He stays for just three days, but when he returns to his homeland he finds himself transported three hundred years into the future.

Urashima Taro

Many years ago on the south coast of Japan there lived a young fisherman called Urashima Taro. He was well-liked by all the people in his village, and when he wasn't fishing, he spent his days caring for his sickly mother. He was also very brave, and would just as likely go out to the sea in a storm as on a calm day, and the locals could not say if he was fearless or foolhardy.

One day, while walking along the sea shore, Urashima Taro saw a knot of children throwing stones at something and laughing. As he approached the children, he saw that they were tormenting a small female turtle. He ran at the youngsters and they scattered before he could catch any of them.

Urashima Taro picked up the turtle and, seeing its shell had protected it against any serious injury, placed it back in the sea.

Day after day for a whole year he continued to fish in all weathers, despite his mother's concern that one day he might never return. One evening, during a particularly fierce storm, his boat was buffeted and blown further and further out to sea. Rain lashed him, and thunder and lightning boomed and flashed all about the boat.

Try as he might, Urashima Taro could not control his boat as the wind and waves did their best to throw him towards a lonely outcrop of black rocks. He was tossed off the boat just as it smashed into the rocks, and he watched as his beloved vessel was smashed to pieces and dragged beneath the waves.

Urashima Taro swam towards the outcrop and clung on to one of the rocks, watching as huge waves boomed and burst all about him. He clung on for what felt like an eternity, but before his weakening arms gave out, he saw something rise from beneath the water's surface.

A giant turtle appeared.

"Urashima Taro," she said, "a year ago you saved my life. "Now climb on my back and let me save yours."

Urashima Taro did not wait, and in a moment he had clambered onto the turtle's back.

"I cannot take you home right now," said the turtle, "the weather is too bad. I will have to take you back to my home in the Palace of the Dragon God."

Urashima Taro barely had time to grab underneath the turtle's shell and hold tight before they began to plunge down into the depths of the ocean. At first he could not breath, and he began to panic. He felt a flicker of pain on either side of his throat, and when he touched his neck, he could feel gills. Now he was able to breath the water as though it was air.

Soon they had swum fathoms down and were on the ocean floor. They were outside a magnificent coral palace, which Urashimo Taro could see was inlaid with gold and silver and colourful gems.

Stepping inside, accompanied by the great turtle, Urashima Taro was met by a beautiful and refined young woman. She wore a shimmering blue dress and a necklace of coloured shells. The turtle introduced them to one another.

"Princess Otohime, this is Urashima Taro – the young man who rescued me from those cruel children."

"You did us all a great service, Urashima Taro," said the Princess.

Urashima Taro was entranced by the Princess's beauty, and she too seemed smitten by the visitor.

"Please do stay with us a while," she said. "I hope our hospitality will go some way towards thanking you for rescuing my turtle."

Urashima Taro was invited to dine, and as he sat down he watched fascinated as fish darted past him.

"How do you find the palace?" said the Princess.

"It is a most beautiful place," Urashima Taro replied.

"Do you think me beautiful?" the Princess asked.

"You are the prettiest woman I have ever seen," he replied. "You are every bit as pretty as the palace you live in."

Urashima Taro had hoped to see the Dragon God during his stay, but that was not to be, and after three days, he said to the Princess: "My love, I must return to my world and see my mother."

"Please do not go," said Princess Otohime. "Stay in my world, where you can become my husband and Prince of this world, and stay young forever."

Urashima Taro shook his head. "My mother is ill, and I fear she only has days to live. I must go back and see her. Love, do not look at me with those sad eyes. I will return the moment I am able."

"If you go, you will never come back," said the Princess.

"Have faith in me, Otohime. When I am ready to return I will call out for your turtle, and she will bring me back."

"I cannot stop you, Urishima Taro, but if you go, you must take this box with you." Princess Otohime handed him a box of coral and jade. "Keep it with you at all times, but promise me you will never open it. Do this and my turtle will meet you on the shore and bring you back."

"I promise," he said.

The Princess bade him farewell.

"Goodbye Princess," he replied, and he climbed on the turtle's back.

Urashima Taro was taken along the sea bed, its gradient rising very slowly. After a few hours of travelling, the sea became so shallow that Urashima Taro was able to jump off the turtle and wade ashore.

Reaching the beach, Urashima Taro stared, puzzled. The shoreline still looked the same – yet something had changed.

The houses are different, he realized.

All the houses that had been there as long as he could remember were gone. Now there were different buildings. Urashima Taro walked to his village. Here too the houses had changed, and only a few that he knew still stood, looking far shabbier than he remembered.

He had known almost every person in his village too, but now every face that looked at him was that of a stranger.

Ahead, he saw his old home, looking very neglected, and he knocked on the door with some trepidation.

An unfamiliar old woman answered.

"Yes?"

Urashima Taro asked if his mother still lived there.

"I've lived here almost eighty years, and my mother and grandmother lived here before me," she replied. "I think you must be mistaken young man."

No person in the village had heard of his mother or any of his friends, and he was directed to a wise old man who might be able to help. The old man listened to Urashima Taro's tale, then thought a moment, as if trying to recall some distant memory.

At last he nodded his head. "Come with me," he said and rose unsteadily to his feet.

He led Urashima Taro out of the village and up a hill towards the cemetery. The area it covered seemed greater than Urashima Taro remembered.

"Check the headstones," said the old man, before turning and leaving the graveyard.

Almost at once Urashima Taro noticed the dates on the newer headstones – it had not been three days since he had last been in this village – it had been almost three hundred years.

"No," he whispered.

As he searched, and the headstones became more aged, he began to notice the names of villagers he had known. Then he came to a weathered slab, located under great tree, and obscured by tall grasses. He pushed the grasses aside and was barely able to read the inscription.

It was his mother's grave. She had died not long after Urashima Taro's last voyage. His name was also written, and underneath it said: Taken by the sea.

Urashima Taro knelt down and wept, and cursed himself bitterly for not listening to his mother when she had implored him not to set sail that stormy evening.

In a fit of despair, he opened the box that Princess Otohime had given him, but to his frustration nothing happened.

He rose and walked back towards the sea in a daze, knowing now that there was nothing for him here and that he should return to the Princess.

Though the beach was not far, he soon found himself beginning to tire. By the time he reached the beach he was barely able to stand, and a moment later he found his legs buckling beneath him. He fell by a rock pool, and when he looked in it he saw his reflection and cried with horror.

Staring back at him was the oldest man he had ever seen, and he could visibly see his reflection – himself – getting older.

He tried to call for the turtle, but his voice barely raised above a croak. He tried again but this time no sound would come. Soon he lay upon the beach and breathed his last, and in less than an hour his body had turned to dust and his ashes were blown out to sea.

And somewhere deep in the ocean Princess Otohime wept.

The Ebony Horse

Introduction

The Ebony Horse was written by an unknown author, possibly of Persian origin circa 900AD, and the tale makes up part of *Arabian Nights*. The ebony horse of the title is a flying machine, upon which Prince Kamar, the story's hero, has a series of adventures.

Rather than simply imbuing the horse with magic, the author used futuristic technology. In this novel story there are mechanisms within the horse, dials to control its flight and it partially inflates before taking off. The ebony horse could therefore be seen not just as a flying machine, but also as a very early portrayal of a robot.

The Ebony Horse

Long ago, there lived a great King called Sabur, and he lived in a splendid palace with his wife, son and three daughters. He was the ruler of all Persia, and was renowned throughout the land for his kindness and wisdom. He was good to his people, comforting those who were distressed, and giving time to those who sought his advice. He also looked after those who had fled from persecution and had sought refuge in his Kingdom. He was hospitable to visitors and generous to the poor, and he was a just man too, with a strong desire to right any wrongs.

Twice a year, Sabur would hold festivals on his palace grounds, once to celebrate the new year, and once to celebrate the Autumn equinox, and people from across Persia, and beyond, would join him to celebrate.

King Sabur was an intelligent man, taking a great interest in science and mathematics, and during one of his festivals he was visited by three inventors who wished to show him their wares.

The first visitor to address him was an Indian, who presented King Sabur with what appeared to be a gold statue, encrusted with gems, and holding a golden trumpet.

"Your Majesty," said the Indian, "this being that I have created will guard your palace against all your enemies. If you place him outside your gates, then

117

when your enemies approach, he will blow the trumpet and your foes will suffer seizures and then death."

The King marvelled at the Indian's work. "If what you have told me is true, then I would happily grant you any wish in return for your creation."

The Indian bowed, and next a Greek inventor came forward. He brought with him a silver dish with a gold peacock in the middle, and twenty four silver chicks about the rim of the dish.

"Oh, mighty King," he began, "as each hour of the day passes, the peacock will turn and peck one of the chicks, so that after one day, all of the chicks will have been pecked. Then, at the end of a lunar month, the peacock will open its beak, and inside you will be able to see the moon."

"That is a fine instrument indeed," said the King, "and I would gladly pay you whatever you asked for it."

The third inventor shuffled forwards. He was an old man of a hundred, with straggling hair and a matted beard. His cheeks were sunken, while his eyes bulged unnaturally. He had three crooked teeth, and in the middle of his wrinkly face was a large, bulbous nose.

He clapped his hands and a horse made of darkest ebony, and inlaid with gold and gemstones trotted into the court. It was fitted with a saddle, bridle and stirrups all made of gold.

"This is my creation," said the old man.

"But how does it walk of its own accord?" asked the King. "Can a person ride it?"

"It can be ridden your Majesty, and not only can my horse trot and canter and gallop – it can fly."

Murmurs broke out through the court, and the Persian craftsman continued. "It can travel through the air, across vast distances and at great speed, and can cover in a single day what others might only be able to in a year."

"By Allah," said the King. "I would give you anything you desire in return for this fine steed."

The King was so impressed by the inventions that he entertained the three wise men for three days, and during that time he witnessed the statue blow its trumpet, and the peacock peck its chicks. The aged Persian inventor mounted the ebony horse and soared high into the air. He flew above the heads of an astonished crowd, before swooping down and landing with ease on the ground.

King Sabur addressed the three sages. "I am amazed by what I have witnessed and believe everything you have told me. Now what gift can I give you in return for your great creations?"

The aged Persian stepped forward and said, "Each of us would like to marry one of your three daughters."

The King did not take long to give his reply. "Your wish is granted."

What neither the King nor the sages knew, was that at this moment the three Princesses were hiding behind a curtain listening to the conversation. The youngest Princess was aghast to hear that she was to be wedded to the ancient Persian, and she ran off to her bedroom, flung herself on her bed, and wept.

Her brother, Prince Kamar, had just returned from a long voyage and knew nothing of the inventors, so as he passed the room of his youngest sister, he was surprised to hear her sobs.

"What's wrong, sister?" he asked.

The Princess sat up, wiped her tears, and recounted her unhappy tale. "Oh brother, I don't wish to marry that horrible old man – but what can I do?"

"I'll talk to father," said Prince Kamar, "and make him see sense."

What neither the Prince nor the Princess knew was at this point the old Persian had overheard their conversation, and scuttled off before the Prince left the room.

Prince Kamar found the King in the open courtyard, and said, "What have you done, father? How can you value a wooden horse above your own daughter?"

The King commanded the servants to bring the horse. "My son," he said, "if you had seen what this horse could do, then you would understand."

The servants brought the horse and Prince Kamar, being an accomplished rider, mounted it, and struck the horse's side with the stirrups.

But the horse did not move. Again the Prince struck the sides of the horse with the stirrups, and again it would not move.

The King called for the inventor, who shuffled into the courtyard.

"Sage," said King Sabur, "show my son how to work this horse."

Having overheard the conversation between the Prince and the Princess, the old man took a dislike to the Prince and now saw an opportunity for revenge.

He approached Prince Kamar. "You see this dial on the right hand side of the horse?"

"Yes," said the Prince.

"You need to turn it."

But no sooner had the Prince done so than the horse shot upwards and vanished from sight.

The King gazed skywards for some time but his son did not return. He ran across to the sage.

"What has happened to my son? Make him return!"

"I cannot, your Majesty," said the sage. "We will not see him now until the Day of Resurrection. Before shooting off into the sky, he was foolish enough not to ask how to land the horse."

The King took off his crown and hurled it at the ground. Then he turned to his guards and pointed at the old man.

"Take him away!" he shouted. "Lock him in jail and throw away the key!"

The King shut himself and his family in the palace, and could not stop his weeping, and when news of this tragedy reached the people of the Kingdom, their happiness turned to grief.

But the Prince was by no means dead. He was soaring through the sky on the ebony horse, in the direction of the sun. Still he could not fathom how to descend.

"There must be a way," he said. "There must!"

He tried the same dial as before, but this only caused the horse to ascend still further and fly at even greater speed. He felt, as far as he was able, over the horse, and found another dial on the horse's left shoulder. With nothing to lose he turned the dial, and the horse began to slow down, and descend towards the Earth.

He found too that the horse had started to respond to

his every touch, the reins turning the horse's head left and right, and causing it to change direction, just like a real horse. Soon Prince Kamar's fear had given way to elation as he realized that he could fly anywhere he wished.

He passed over fields and woods, mountains and rivers, villages and cities, and was amazed by the magnificent views. As the sun was beginning to set, he realized he would never make it home before dark, so he took to setting down in the next town.

Prince Kamar flew over the walls of a splendid city without any of the guards that surrounded it noticing, and he settled the horse on the terrace roof of a palace.

Jumping off the horse, he turned to the wooden creature and said, "The man who made you was a clever man indeed – and a cunning one too. Let us hope that we are able to return home soon."

The sky was now inky blue, and the first few stars beginning to twinkle. Having not had anything to eat or drink since the morning, Prince Kamar left the horse, descended a nearby staircase, and found himself in a fine courtyard paved with marble.

It was deserted and eerily quiet. He wandered along the moonlit path around the palace's perimeter. After a minute of walking he noticed a chink of light and saw that a palace side-door was ajar.

Leaning against the door frame was a eunuch, guarding the entrance, but as Prince Kamar approached he heard the guard's soft snores. The Prince took the sleeping guard's sword, snuck inside, and found some food and water which he devoured gratefully. Being of an adventurous spirit, the Prince ventured further inside the palace.

Sneaking through one of the many doors, he entered a room where, in the middle, he saw four servant girls lying around a bed of ivory and jewels.

The Prince crept past the servant girls and saw that on the bed lay a beautiful young woman. She had fair skin, and soft red cheeks, and was so beautiful that Kamar could not help but lean over and kiss her.

Her eyes opened.

"Who are you?" she asked.

"I am your love, and your slave," said the Prince.

"You must be the suitor whom my father rejected," said the lady, rubbing her eyes. "My father said you were an ugly and unpleasant man, but you seem to be neither of those."

The slaves awoke to see their mistress talking to the stranger.

"Princess – who is this man?" one of them asked.

"I don't know," said the young woman. "When I awoke, he was seated by my bed. I believe he is the suitor my father rejected."

"No," replied the slave girl. "I saw your suitor – he looked like some grotesque creature, and his manners were terrible."

The four maidens went outside and saw the eunuch sleeping. They woke him and said, "how did you let a men get through and wake us from our sleep?"

The eunuch ran inside and shouted at the Prince. "How did you sneak past me?" he blustered. "Did you bewitch me? Are you some sort of demon?"

"How dare you compare me to such an evil creature. I am your King's son-in-law. I have married his daughter, and he has asked me to visit her."

The eunuch frowned. "I beg your pardon, my lord," said the eunuch. "I meant no disrespect."

Blushing, the eunuch retreated and then ran to the King.

Suspicious of the Prince's words, the eunuch told the King of what he had seen. "You will need to rescue your daughter from this evil demon, this abomination that has taken on the appearance of a handsome and noble man."

"You fool," said the King. "How did you let him slip past?"

"He must have bewitched me, sire."

The King marched to his daughter's bedroom, and addressed the servant girls.

"What has become of my daughter?" he asked.

"Your Majesty," they replied, "sleep overcame us all, and when we woke we saw a young man sitting on the edge of Princess Shams bed, and talking to her. We asked him who he was, and he said that you had given him your daughter's hand in marriage. We knew nothing of this, and we did not know if he was a man or a spirit, but he is modest and well-bred, and has done nothing untoward."

When the King heard this, his anger cooled, and he passed through a curtain into an adjacent room where his daughter was sitting, talking to the Prince.

Once more the King's anger grew and, unable to control his temper, he charged at the Prince, who leapt up, sword in hand.

"Is this your father?" Prince Kamar asked the lady.

"Yes," she replied.

The King was no match for the Prince, and in the end the King, knowing he could not defeat the youth, put his sword back in its sheath.

"Young man," he said. "Are you the noble man that you appear to be, or are you some evil spirit who has bewitched my household?"

"If I was a demon, I would not have spared you. I am Prince Kamar, son of King Sabur of Persia."

"But if you are a noble Prince, then how did you enter my palace? Why did you come without an invitation, or even request to be invited? Why did you enter my daughter's room, and why did you say that I had given you her hand in marriage? And if I called out now and my guards came rushing in, who would be able to save you from a dozen sharp swords? Who could save you?"

"Do you think that someone as brave as handsome as I am, is unworthy of marriage to your daughter?"

"It is not just about looks and bravery. Your coming here, to my daughter's room, in such a manner, is hardly befitting of a Prince."

"That is true, but calling your guards and having them kill me will only cause great trouble for you. People will surely ask what I was doing in your daughter's bedroom. And while many may believe what you say, many will not. So let me give you some words of wisdom."

The King folded his arms. "Pray tell," he said.

"You could fight me in armed combat, here and now, or I could take on your entire army. But first you will need to tell me how many men you have."

"More than forty thousand."

"Tomorrow morning you can tell them that they must take me on. Tell them also that if I am slain, so be it, and if I rout them, then I am to have your daughter's hand in marriage. If I am slain, the secret is taken to my grave, and if I succeed, then any King should be happy to have me as his son-in-law."

The King thought for a few moments, and then accepted Prince Kamar's proposition.

The next morning, as the soldiers put on their armour and mounted their horses, the Prince and the King spoke at length. The King found Prince Kamar to be an intelligent man and of good breeding, and as the Prince left to do battle, the King said: "Take any of my horses that you wish."

"The only horse I shall ride into battle, is the one that brought me here."

"And where is this horse?"

"Your palace."

"Don't be absurd," said the King. "If your horse was there, my guards would have told me. Whereabouts in the palace?"

"Up on the roof."

"Are you mocking me, Prince? Well, no matter, we shall see." The King turned to one of his generals. "Go to the palace roof and bring me anything you might find."

The people nearest were amazed by the very notion. "How could a horse have ascended the steps?" they asked. "How on Earth will anyone be able to lead it back down?"

The soldier took some of his men with him and they soon found the horse. When they realised it was made of ebony and not a real horse, they laughed.

"Is this the horse he rode into town?" said the general.

"We'll soon find out," said one of the soldiers, and together they lifted the horse and carried it down the steps.

When they set it down before the King, he marvelled at the workmanship.

"Prince Kamar," he said, "is this really your horse?"

"It is, your majesty, and soon I will show it to you in all its glory."

"Very well," said the King, "mount your horse."

"Not until your troops withdraw some way from it."

The King ordered his troops to withdraw so far that the horse was just out of the bowmen's range.

"Do not spare the lives of any of my men," said the King, "for they certainly will not spare yours."

Prince Kamar leapt onto his horse and sat facing an almost uncountable number of soldiers.

They stared back at this solitary figure.

"When he comes near, we can run him through with our pikes, and then chop him to pieces with our swords," said one soldier.

"It doesn't seem right, slaying that young man," said another.

"I don't think slaying him will be that easy – he managed to get into the city and then into the palace without so much as a scratch."

The Prince slowly turned the ascent dial. The horse shuddered, and Prince Kamar saw the creature's belly fill with air. He and his steed began to rise, slowly at first, and then Kamar and the horse shot up into the sky.

The King cried aloud. "Chase after him – he didn't want the horse to fight a battle, he wanted it to escape!"

Prince Kamar flew out over the city walls, waving as he left.

"Follow him!" the King ordered, as the Prince flew away.

But his council of wise men said, "There is no way the Prince and his flying horse can be caught. Look, he's already but a speck on the horizon. He is surely a mighty wizard – be thankful he has left without using his powers upon you and your subjects."

The King returned to his palace and explained what had happened to his daughter.

Princess Shams broke down, and began to sob.

The King put his arms round the Princess and tried to console her.

"There, there, my daughter," he said. "Be thankful that we are free from this deceitful sorcerer who came here to seduce you. Remember all the lies he spoke – do not let your heart break over such a scoundrel."

But Princess Shams would not listen to her father. "I will not eat and I will not drink until I meet with my Prince once more."

"My daughter, do not speak of such things."

But the more the King tried to talk to his daughter, the stronger her love grew for the Prince.

At this moment Prince Kamar rejoiced at having escaped, and felt exhilarated as he flew through the air. But his joy was dampened when he thought of the beautiful Princess he had left behind. On the way home he landed and enquired about the city he had left, and was told its name was Sana.

The journey home seemed quicker than his unplanned trip to Sana, and when he saw his father's capital, his heart filled with joy. He circled round the city before alighting on the palace roof.

He descended the steps, and saw ashes strewn across the entrance – a sign that someone in the family had died. He entered to see his mother, father and sisters dressed in black, consoling one another.

The King turned and saw his son.

"No," said the King, "it cannot be!"

Soon Prince Kamar found himself being embraced by all his family. They had all thought him dead and were overjoyed that their mourning had been unnecessary.

Prince Kamar recounted his adventure to his happy family, and the King decided to hold a great festival across Persia to celebrate his son's return. The population cast off their mourning clothes, and dressed themselves in their most colourful garments. Streets were decorated, and parties were held in every town. The King proclaimed that all prisoners should be pardoned, and every prisoner in the country was released, and for seven days and nights celebrations took place across the land.

He and his son took their finest horses and rode through towns and villages, so the people might see the Prince.

"What became of the sage who created the ebony horse?" asked the Prince.

"I threw him in prison, but as you are alive and well, I shall release him as I have released all prisoners."

After they had spent the day riding through joyous crowds, they returned to the palace, and the King sent for the sage. The old man was treated with utmost kindness, and was given food and drink and new clothes.

"Your Highness, I was promised that I could marry your daughter –"

"Hold your tongue," said the King. "You will not marry her after what you did to my son. Be thankful that you are no longer in chains."

"But you made a promise!" the sage cried. "Your daughter should now be my wife!"

"Get him out," said the King, and two soldiers dragged the old sage, and threw him out of the palace gates, then locked them so he could not get back in.

"My son," said the King, "you would do well to steer clear of that man's strange horse. I doubt you know all of its capabilities, and I can hardly bear the thought of you flying away again."

The Prince told his father about the King of Sana, and Princess Shams, and felt the pang of separation as he spoke of her. A female singer took to performing in front of the royal family and their guests. She played her stringed instrument with great skill, and when she sang of separated lovers, the Prince asked that he might leave the room for a while.

Prince Kamar was overwhelmed with yearning for his distant Princess, and he decided, in spite of what his father had told him, that he had to see her again.

He ascended the steps to the palace roof and

mounted his black wooden horse. He turned the ascent dial, and soon he was in the air, flying back towards the city he had only recently escaped.

The next morning the King realized his son had disappeared once more, and after a quick search of the castle it was found that the horse had gone too.

"If my son comes back to me," the King said to himself, "I'll make sure I destroy that infernal horse." And he broke down and wept.

The Prince though was in a cheery mood, and he did not stop at any point on his long flight until he reached the city of Sana, and once more alighted on the palace roof. He crept down the stairs and past the eunuch who was asleep again. When he reached the door to Princess Sana's bedroom, Prince Kamar heard her weeping.

One of the servant girls said, "Why do you mourn for a someone who never loved you?"

But the Princess continued to cry, and Prince Kamar could not remain outside the room a moment longer.

"Why do you weep, my love?" said the Prince.

Princess Sana, threw her arms about the Prince and kissed him. "I thought I would never see you again," she replied.

"I had to come back and see you," said the Prince.

"If you had stayed away a day longer," said Princess Shams, "I think I would have died of grief."

"I hope your father does not try to come between us," said Prince Kamar. "Had it not been for my love for you, I would have run him through with my sword."

"Why did you leave me, my love?"

"I had to, but only for a while. Let us not dwell on such things now, I'm hungry and thirsty."

The servant girls brought him food and drink, and he and Princess Shams sat talking well into the night.

When dawn broke, the Prince said, "I should leave before the eunuch guard wakes."

"Where will you go?" said the Princess.

"Back to my father's palace," the Prince replied, and on seeing the dismay and sadness in her eyes, added. "I will come back to see you every week, and I pledge now that you will be my only love, always and forever."

But his words could not stem her weeping. "Why not take me with you?"

"Would you do that?" he replied. "Would you come with me back to my father's palace?"

"My life is worthless without you," said the Princess. "Please let me come."

"Then let us not waste another moment," said the Prince.

Princess Shams adorned herself with her most cherished jewels, said goodbye to her maidens, and followed Prince Kamar onto the palace roof. She sat on the ebony horse, behind the Prince, and put her arms tightly about his waist. Prince Kamar turned the ascent dial, and soon they were rising into the air.

When the maidens saw their mistress flying off, they were so shocked that they cried aloud and ran to tell Princess Shams' mother and father. The King and Queen ran outside to see their daughter flying away, and the King cried aloud. "In the name of Allah, bring our daughter back to us you evil spirit!"

The Prince, worried that the Princess might be having second thoughts, said, "Do you wish me to return you to your parents?"

"No – fly on!" replied the Princess. "My only wish is to be with you."

The Prince flew the horse at a moderate pace, so as not to frighten the Princess, and they alighted in a green field where a fresh water river cut through. They sat and ate and drank, and after they had rested, they took off once more, flying on until they could see King Sabur's palace.

Prince Kamar could not wait to show Princess Shams the splendour of his father's Kingdom, and the beautiful palace where his family lived, and when he approached one of his father's gardens, just outside the city, he turned the descent dial so they floated downwards and landed softly.

"Wait here, my love," said the Prince, leaving the Princess and the ebony horse. "I will let my father know you have come, and I will send a servant to escort you inside when everything is ready."

The Princess understood that as a member of a royal family, she should not enter the city without first being invited by the King.

The King was glad to see his son safe and well, and said nothing of his sadness at his son having left the palace.

"I have brought Princess Shams with me," said the Prince. "She is outside the city walls in one of your gardens. I hope you will welcome her to our city."

"With all my heart!" exclaimed the King, and he collected the most important people within the city and together they rode out to welcome the Princess.

Meanwhile the Prince set up decorations within the palace and gathered together servant girls to tend to all Princess Shams' needs. Then he set out to join his father and his love. But when he reached the gardens Princess Shams was not there. She had disappeared, and so had the horse.

"What has happened?" he said to his father. "Where is she?"

"The guards say that the Persian sage came through the entrance to collect herbs, but never left the garden as far as they could tell."

"He's taken her!" cried the Prince. "I will search for her, and I'll not come back until I have found her again."

"But you will never be able to find her," said the King. "Come home with us now. Do not spend the rest of your life searching in vain."

But the Prince would not listen to his father. His feelings for Princess Sana were far too strong.

When the Prince had left the Princess in the garden, the sage, quite by chance had gone there to collect herbs, as the guards had reported. His bulbous nose gave him a keen sense of smell, and when he sniffed the air he could sense some exquisite perfumes. So he followed his nose, until he spied the Princess standing by the horse that he had built.

He had mourned the loss of his horse and thought, until now, that he would never see it again. Now his heart leapt with delight. He approached the Princess, who could not help but shrink back at the sight of such a hideous looking man.

"Who are you?" she asked.

The sage knew she was of royal blood by her countenance, and that she must be waiting to be let into the city.

"I am a messenger, my lady," he said. "Prince Kamar has asked me to escort you into the city."

"Could he have not found someone more handsome to escort me?" she said.

"The Prince sent the ugliest servant he could find because he has a jealous nature," said the sage, "and thought that if he sent someone more handsome, you might elope."

They talked some more, and the cunning sage was able to convince the Princess that she had made a grave mistake in coming here with the Prince.

"You should leave here as quickly as possible," said the old man. "Or you will face a life of utter misery, just like his other wives."

"But how shall we leave?"

"On this horse."

"But I do not know how to fly it."

"Do not worry yourself, my lady," said the sage, "I know how to control its movements."

So the old man sat on the horse, and Princess Shams sat behind him, and soon they were flying through the air.

It suddenly dawned on the Princess that the Prince would be unlikely to send a man who would so easily betray him.

"Why did you disobey your Prince?" she asked.

"He is not my Prince," snapped the old man. "He is little more than a well-dressed snake. Do you know who I am?"

"No – I thought you were one of the Prince's servants."

"Well I'm not his servant and never have been. He's an arrogant young upstart, and his father is a wicked and unjust man, who stole my horse and threw me in prison."

"Your horse – the one we're riding now?"

"Of course," said the sage. "I made it myself and thought I'd lost it forever. But now I have it back, and I have you, and I hope it causes the Prince and his family more suffering than they caused me. You shall be my wife, in place of the King's daughter. Your life will not be a bad one if you marry me. I am clever and I am wealthy, and I have plenty of slaves that will serve you."

"Take me back to the Prince at once!"

But the Sage took no notice, he wasn't going to lose a wife for a second time.

Princess Shams wept for the whole journey, until they reached Greece and alighted in a meadow filled with streams and trees. In the not too far distance was a beautiful city where a King lived, and it happened that at this moment, the King was out hunting and saw the old sage and the Princess.

The King's servants brought the Princess and the old man to their master.

The King eyed the ugly old sage and the beautiful young Princess.

"What is the relationship between you?" the King asked the sage. "Is she your granddaughter?"

"What should you care?" growled the sage. "Just

because you're dressed in all your finery you think you can harass a poor old man." said the sage. "Well if you really must know, she is my wife, and, as it happens, the daughter of my father's brother."

"He is not my husband!" the Princess exclaimed. "He's a wicked old man, who has kidnapped me!"

The King believed the Princess, and the Persian sage was beaten by the King's soldiers, taken back to the King's city and thrown into jail. Then the King escorted the Princess and the ebony horse back to his palace.

Prince Kamar grabbed some money and all that he needed to travel, and set off in search of his beloved Princess. He journeyed from city to city and from country to country, asking people if they had seen Princess Shams or the ebony horse. But all his searches and questions appeared to be in vain – no one could give him even a scrap of information. He even visited the Princess's father, but even here there was no news, and so Prince Kamar left the mourning King.

The Prince, having covered the whole of Persia, and having had no luck, made for Greece, where his enquiries at last proved fruitful.

It happened that he came across a group of merchants, who were talking among themselves.

"You'll never believe what I saw," said one of them.

"Come on," said another. "Tell us."

"I was visiting the King's city, and heard the strangest tale. The King was out hunting when he came to a green meadow, and came across an ugly old man, a beautiful young woman and an ebony horse."

"And then what?"

"The old man claimed that the woman was his wife and cousin, but she told the King that the old man was lying and that he'd kidnapped her. The King threw the old man in jail, but I couldn't tell you what became of the young woman or the ebony horse."

Prince Kamar approached the storyteller.

"Pray, tell me the name of this city and where I might find it," he asked.

The merchant happily gave the Prince all the information that was requested, but as it was late the Prince stayed at some lodgings and did not set off until first light the following morning.

After a few hours travel on his trusty horse, Prince Kamar reached the entrance to the King's metropolis. The gatekeepers had been told by the King to bring him any stranger that might visit the city, and so they escorted Prince Kamar to the palace. Here the King would normally ask any stranger to state their reason for visiting, but on this occasion the King was dining and would not be disturbed, so the gatekeepers put the Prince in the hands of the prison guards.

The guards could not believe that such a handsome and refined young man could mean any harm, so they let him dine with them.

"Where are you from?" one of the guards asked.

"Persia," the Prince replied. "From the land of the Chosroes."

The guard laughed. "Well that's a coincidence – you're not the only Chosroan in this prison."

"It's true," said the other guard. "There's an ugly old man, who was probably just as ugly when he was young. Everything he says is either unpleasant, or a downright lie."

"What lies has he told?"

"He said he was a wise man. When the King found him in a meadow, the old man was with a beautiful young lady and an ebony horse. He said the woman was his wife, when she wasn't. It turns out he'd kidnapped her, and so the King threw him in prison."

"What has become of the Princess?" said Prince Kamar.

The guard shook his head. "She's gone mad. The King wants to marry her, but can't so long as she's in this state. The old man was asked to cure her, but he couldn't. The King has employed the finest physicians and astrologers to cure her, but no one's been able."

The other guard spoke: "The horse is somewhere in the King's palace. The old man is here with us in the prison, and at night he wails and cries so loudly that we're kept awake until dawn."

When it was time to sleep, the Prince allowed himself to be escorted back to his prison cell, and he lay upon a bed of straw. The guards locked him in, and bade him goodnight.

Soon, just as the guards had said, he heard the Persian sage weeping and crying aloud.

"What a fool I've been!" he sobbed. "Why did I steal that beautiful young woman away when I knew I had no chance of making her my wife? I have left the Prince without the woman he loves, and now I'm stuck in this miserable place! Oh, what have I done?"

The Prince called back. "Old sage," he shouted. "How long are you going to weep for? Do you think that you are the only person who suffers? There are others who have a harder time than you, but do not complain of their lot."

Still the sage moaned, but the Prince, to his own surprise, began to pity the ugly old man.

The next morning the Prince was taken from his cell and directly to the King.

"Where are you from," asked the King, "and why have you come here?"

"My name is Harjah" said Prince Kamar, "and I am from Persia. I am a wise man who travels around healing the sick, especially those who have been possessed and driven to madness by malevolent spirits. To this day I have never failed to heal a patient."

The King clapped his hands delightedly. "Sage," he exclaimed, "you do not know what happiness your words have brought me! Never has a person come at a more appropriate time. Praise be to Allah!"

The King then told Prince Kamar about the Princess and her affliction.

"If you cure her, I shall give you anything you want."

"Let us hope that Allah looks upon this case favourably," said the Prince. "Tell me all you know of her affliction, how long she has suffered from it, and how she came to be with the horse and the old man."

The King recounted the whole story faithfully, in every detail.

"And where is the old man now?" asked the Prince.

"He is in jail."

"And what about the ebony horse?"

"It has been stowed away in one of my treasure chambers."

"First, I will need to see the horse and check its condition," said the Prince. "If it is in good condition I believe it can help the poor young woman."

"Yes, of course," said the King. "I can take you to see the horse immediately."

"Lead the way," said the Prince.

So the King led the Prince to the treasure chamber. Prince Kamar examined the horse in minute detail, as the King looked on.

"It seems fine," the Prince said at last. "Let us go and visit the damsel, and see if we can cure her."

So together they visited the Princess, who was in her bedroom. The Prince saw her sitting on the ground, rocking back and forth, crying, and beating the ground with her fists. Then she began to claw at her dress and rip it shreds. But she was not mad, she feigned this affliction so that people – not least the King – would be too scared to approach her.

"I mean you no harm," said Prince Kamar, not knowing if she really was insane.

Through her tears and distress the Princess did not realize that it was the Prince who addressed her.

When he knelt by her side he whispered in her ear. "It is I, Prince Kamar."

The moment Princess Shams heard these words she cried out and fainted.

The King thought the Princess had, through fear of the stranger, suffered a seizure.

The Prince picked her up and said as quietly as possible. "Shams, I hope you can hear me. I've come to help you escape from the King. I have told him I am a sage who has come to cure you. I will tell him that to drive away the spirit that possesses you, he will first have to let you leave his castle. I want you speak to him kindly whenever he talks to you, so that he thinks that I've cured you."

She opened her eyes. "Very well my love," she said, and sat up.

"Your majesty," said the Prince, " I have discovered the cause of her disease, and have cured her. Come and talk to her with kindness. There will be a little more to do, but I believe the worst is over."

The King approached her with caution, but when she looked up and saw him, Princess Shams smiled.

"Thank you for visiting me," she said.

The King, seeing that she was no longer raving, felt his heart skip with joy, and he bade his servants to escort her to a better room and dress her in the finest clothes and jewellery.

As she was bathed by female servants, she made polite conversation with them, then she was dressed and adorned with beautiful jewels. Then she was escorted to the King where she kissed the ground before him.

"Wise sage!" the King said happily, "You have done a great deed! I must be the happiest person in the Kingdom!"

"There is still more work to be done," Prince Kamar said solemnly. "Bring me the ebony horse," he said. "The spirit that possessed this woman, came from that horse and has undoubtedly returned there. Unless I banish the spirit from the horse, he will return and possess the woman once more."

"I will do it at once," said the King, and he

commanded his servants to bring the horse.

"We shall all go to the meadow where you found her," said the Prince.

So the King, Prince Kamar and Princess Shams rode out to the meadow, while the servants carried the ebony horse.

The Prince turned to the King. "This will be a dangerous affair," he said grimly. "You and the servants will need to keep well back."

"How far?" asked the King.

"Until we are specks in the distance," said the Prince. "I will have to banish the spirit, and then imprison him so that he can never harm another human being. Then I will have to mount the horse with the lady. After this the horse will begin to rock, then it will fly through the air towards you, and then all shall be well and you can do as you wish with the damsel."

So the King retreated so he could barely see what what was going on. He saw the Prince and Princess mount the ebony horse, then he saw them take off into the sky. For half a day he waited for them to return, and then he began to grieve.

Frustrated at being duped, he returned to the palace with his servants, and summoned the old man.

"You treacherous swine! Why didn't you tell me the properties of the ebony horse!" he cried. "Now a man even more cunning you has taken the horse, and the woman I loved. And if that wasn't bad enough, she was wearing some of the finest jewels that my soldiers have plundered!"

The old man recounted the whole tale truthfully from beginning to end, and in his despair the King suffered a seizure that almost ended his life.

The King was taken to his bed chamber and over the next few days, with the aid of his physicians, he eventually recovered.

"Sire," said one of his wise men, "be thankful that you are rid of that woman who undoubtedly was some sort of witch, and praise Allah that the sorcerer that took her away did no more damage."

Eventually these soothing words comforted the King, and soon he was happily seeking out a new bride.

The Prince and Princess flew back to Persia, and to King Sabur's palace. They alighted on the roof, and Prince Kamar left the Princess in the company of the horse.

He found his mother and father and together they rejoiced at their reunion, then the Prince explained that he had brought Princess Shams with him, and they were cheered to hear that he had found his love and had brought her back with him.

Great banquets were laid out for all the people of the capital, and there were celebrations for a whole month, culminating in the marriage of the royal couple.

King Sabur smashed the ebony horse, breaking all the mechanisms within it that gave it the ability to fly, and though Prince Kamar was sad to see this, he understood why it had been done.

Prince Kamar wrote to the Princess's father, explaining the whole tale and telling him of the marriage, and he sent a messenger along with some very fine gifts. When the messenger reached the city of Sana, and delivered the gifts and the letter, the King was rejoiced to hear that his daughter was happy and well. He gathered together gifts of his own and gave them to the messenger to take to his daughter and son-in-law.

Every year Prince Kamar would send the King letters and gifts, and in time Prince Kamar became King, and Princess Shams became Queen, and, just as King Sabur had done, they ruled together justly and wisely for the rest of their lives.

The City of Brass

Introduction

The City of Brass was written by an unknown author, possibly of Persian origin circa 900AD, and the story makes up part of *Arabian Nights*. In this tale a group of travellers come upon a walled ghost town with no discernible entrance. When they are eventually able to enter the city, among their strange encounters, they come across automata and a mummified queen. This is a fantasy tale in the main, but is included in this anthology as it contains some elements of science fiction.

The City of Brass

Long ago there lived a Caliph by the name of Malik.
He was very interested in myths and legends, and one
day, while talking with kings and sultans, their
conversation turned to an old tale of how King
Solomon had managed to imprison spirits and demons
in stoppered bottles.

A young man named Talib, who was present in this
conversation, knew of this tale and said, "My
grandfather once captained a ship that was blown far
off course by a great storm. They ran aground and
after journeying for some months, they reached the
foot of some great mountains. Here they came across a
tribe of black-skinned people. None of them spoke
Arabic, but fortunately, the king of the tribe was sent
for, and he was able to converse a little with my
grandfather. The king welcomed the crew and
entertained them for three days. On the fourth day, my
grandfather was taken fishing, but among the fish
contained in one particular net was a blue, stoppered
bottle. The fishermen and my grandfather returned to
shore, where a sailor smashed the bottle against some
rocks, shattering it into a thousand pieces. A genie
billowed out, looking like smoke, and grew until he
was as high as the clouds.

"'Oh, Allah!' the Genie cried. 'Allah, I am sorry for
all the wickedness I have done!'

"After that, the genie disappeared. The king told my

grandfather and his crew that local fishermen often dredged up these bottles, and broke them open to release some repenting spirit."

The Caliph was amazed by Talib's strange tale.

"Talib," he said, "you must travel to Morocco and meet with Musa the Emir, and together you shall go on a journey to seek out these strange bottles."

So Talib made the long journey to Morocco and met with Musa, where he explained the Caliph's wish. Talib and Musa the Emir set off in the company of a wise Sheikh called Samad, and took with them plenty of men, camels and provisions.

The Sheikh had heard of this legend and had some idea of the way to the base of these great mountains by the sea. He explained that they should follow the coast, and that the journey should take around four months.

To begin with they made good progress, with the Sheikh using the stars to plot their journey. But after a few cloudy nights, when none of the stars could be seen, they wandered off course.

For days they saw nothing, and their first sight of human habitation was a great, bejewelled palace.

"My grandfather also came across a palace like this one," said Talib, "and after this he came across another place called the City of Brass, which he was unable to enter."

The bejewelled palace was deserted, and the Sheikh read a scroll that explained how Death had visited this wondrous place. The king at the time had tried to bargain with Death, offering up all his treasures for one more day of life. But Death would not bargain, and the king died at his appointed time.

So Talib, the Emir, the Sheikh and their men left the palace, and continued their journey across the barren lands. After a few days of monotony they saw, in the distance, a man on his horse, and they decided to approach him. But he was no ordinary man. Indeed he wasn't really a man at all, for he, and his horse, were made of brass.

At the base of this metal statue some words were inscribed:

'Touch the hand of this rider, and he will point you in the direction of the City of Brass.'

Talib touched the hot metal hand. A moment passed when all was still and quiet, then a creaking noise sounded. The horse turned as though on a revolving plate, then stopped. The rider's arm raised stiffly, and his finger pointed.

Leaving this mysterious statue, the party took the direction given to them by the horseman, and after a journey of many days they came to the city.

"Where is the entrance?" asked the Emir, looking up and along the city's high, golden wall.

Talib took a company of twenty five men round the entire perimeter, and after three days they returned, full circle, back to their companions.

"We've searched every part of the wall," said Talib. "There is no way in. It doesn't make sense."

"I have heard," said the Sheikh that there are twenty five portals, none of which can be opened from outside the city."

"Then how are we supposed to enter?" said Talib.

The Sheikh replied, "I do not know."

"If we cannot go through," said the Emir, "then

perhaps we could try going over the top. We have enough materials to make a tall ladder."

Over the next few days a tall, sturdy ladder was made, then lifted and lent against the city wall.

There were no shortage of volunteers to climb the ladder and see if there was any way down into the city. Eventually one soldier, renowned for his courage and ability, was allowed to climb to the top of the city wall.

"What can you see?" called the Emir.

But the soldier did not reply. He just stared down into the city with a faint smile on his face – and then he jumped, screaming as he fell.

"The journey must have taken its toll on him more than we ever suspected," said Talib.

A second soldier was sent up the ladder, and he too stood at the top of the wall, staring down the other side.

"What do you see?" shouted the Emir.

The soldier, like the last, did not reply, and before anyone could act, the man jumped into the city to the horror of his companions.

A third soldier was sent up and he too jumped to his death, and so it continued until a dozen soldiers had perished in the same manner.

"Let me go next," said the Sheikh.

"No," said the Emir, "absolutely not. If we lose you, our quest is at an end."

"I promise you, Emir, Allah will not desert me."

Eventually, after much discussion, the Emir allowed the old Sheikh to ascend the ladder.

As he climbed, the Sheikh prayed all the while, and

when he reached the top of the wall, he stepped upon the wide metal plateau, and gazed down into the city.

Below, there was a deep lake of water, or so it seemed, shimmering and glistening in the sunlight. Around the edge of the lake were twelve beautiful maidens, encouraging him to jump into the cool, sparkling lake. But the Sheikh resisted their tempting calls, and as he continued to pray, the lake began to fade, and he could see the broken bodies of the twelve soldiers.

Knowing they could not tempt him, the maidens vanished, and the lake disappeared. The Sheikh walked along the wide top of the wall until he came to a turret with no visible entrance. In front of the wall was a brass horseman, not unlike the one that had directed the Sheikh and his companions to the City of Brass. There was an inscription at the base of this metal statue:

'Whoever wishes to enter the City of Brass must turn the dial in the middle of my chest twelve times.'

There was a dial and with some effort the Sheikh turned it. The Sheikh stepped back as sparks began to fly, and the horseman began to rotate. As it turned a door began to open.

The Sheikh passed through the entrance, and descended a staircase until he found himself in a dusty old room, filled with skeletons. On the wall was a set of keys, which he took. He left the room and walked along the inside of the city wall until he came to a great brass door, which he knew to be quite invisible from the other side.

He put the largest key in the lock and turned it. The

door, of its own accord, began to creak open, and soon the Sheikh was face-to-face with his companions once more.

As they explored the city, they found not a living soul. They found many skeletons dressed in rags, there were skeletons in the houses and in the market place, as though Death had come swiftly to the city and caught its inhabitants off guard.

Talib, the Emir, the Sheikh and a handful of soldiers entered one particularly fine building, a palace made of gold and silver. Inside there were beautifully carved pieces of furniture, draped in silk, and there were fine paintings and ornaments made of the most precious gems. They explored the whole building and were amazed by the treasures they saw. But when they came to the end of one long, wide corridor, they found that the door would not open. It was a particularly fine door made of ebony and inlaid with gold. The Emir looked at the door, but there seemed to be no way of opening it and there appeared to be no lock. The Sheikh spent some time putting his hands on different parts of the door. He said that he knew what he was doing, and eventually the door clicked open.

The small group passed into what was undoubtedly the most splendid room in the palace. It was made of marble, and much of the stone was decorated with sapphires and diamonds and emeralds. There was a bird made of rubies, and on the couch lay a young woman. Of all the jewels in the city, the finest adorned her. She wore a silk robe, inlaid with pearls, a red-gold crown sparkling with gems, a jewelled amulet on her breast, and a necklace of rubies and emeralds. To her left and right, flanking her couch, were two statues of slaves, one black and one white, and each with a sword in his hand.

At first the Emir thought the young woman was still alive, but Talib was less certain.

"She has been mummified," said the Sheikh. "Mercury was put behind her eyes to make them glisten, and the air blows her eyelashes, giving them a sense of movement."

In the woman's hand was a piece of paper, which the Sheikh took and read aloud to his companions.

"Welcome to those whom Allah has let into my city. Take any treasure you wish, but pray leave those treasures that adorn me."

"But she is dead," said Talib, staring longingly at the glittering jewels the dead young woman wore. "She has no need of them now."

Before anyone could stop him, Talib stepped forwards and reached out to grab the woman's crown. The moment his fingers touched it, the black statue swung his sword and sliced Talib's head clean off.

"Come," said the Sheikh, "let us leave this place. We still have the Caliph's task to complete."

The Emir and the soldiers loaded their camels with treasures from the City of Brass, and continued their journey. After a month of travelling, they came across some mountains overlooking the sea. They were welcomed by black-skinned people who lived there and spoke a quite different language. The king of these people, however, was able to speak Arabic, and he conversed with the Sheikh and the Emir.

The Emir said, "We have been sent by Malik the

Caliph, to find bottles in which King Solomon imprisoned demons and spirits. We have journeyed many months in the hope of finding these items."

"Then you have reached your destination," said the king.

He showed his guests great hospitality, letting them rest for many days. After a week, his fishermen had managed to find a dozen such bottles, which the Emir and Sheikh took back to the Caliph.

The Caliph, upon receiving the bottles, smashed some of them open, releasing many repentant spirits. Then he sent more men to the City of Brass, to recover treasures, which he divided among the faithful.

The Tale of the Bamboo Cutter

Introduction

The Tale of the Bamboo Cutter was written by an unknown Japanese author around the tenth century AD. This beautiful tale, blending romance and science fiction, tells of a girl found as a baby amongst some bamboo. As she grows, she reveals that she is a Princess exiled from the Moon. Eventually her people come in their spacecraft to take her home. This is the earliest known story to tell of extraterrestrials visiting the Earth.

The Tale of the Bamboo Cutter

Long ago there lived an old bamboo cutter. He and his wife were very poor, and to their dismay they had never been blessed with children. The old man toiled each day in his bamboo field, earning just enough to live on by cutting down and selling the shoots.

One evening however, when his day's toil was coming to a close, he noticed a fabulous light shining nearby. Hacking his way through the shoots, he soon came across the source of this strange glow – a baby girl, small enough to fit on the palm of his hand. The bamboo cutter picked up the girl and took her home. He and his wife were delighted at the prospect of raising the child, and they blessed the girl with the name Lady Kaguya.

From this day, whenever the bamboo cutter went into his field to work, he found a small nugget of gold in every stalk that he cut, and within a month he and his wife had become very rich. But this was not the only strange occurrence, for Lady Kaguya developed at such speed, that after just a few months she had grown to the height of an ordinary human. She was also very beautiful, and she was soon reckoned to be the prettiest young woman in the country, causing men from far and wide to come and see her for themselves.

The bamboo cutter soon became wearied by the young men's demands to see Lady Kaguya, and his attempts to send them away only met with limited success. While other men relented, five noblemen could not be persuaded to leave, and all pleaded with the bamboo cutter to let them marry his beautiful daughter. The bamboo cutter explained that as she was not really his child, it was up to her whether or not she wished to marry any of them.

Eventually Lady Kaguya agreed to meet the five noblemen. She set each of them a near-impossible task, and said that she would marry the first man to complete his task successfully.

The first nobleman was told that he must travel to India and bring back a stone begging bowl that had been used by Buddha himself; the second nobleman was told he must travel to a distant land where he had to find a tree with gold branches, silver roots, and fruit of pure jade, and bring Lady Kaguya one of the tree's branches; the third was asked to find a magical robe made from the pelts of flame-proof rats; the fourth was told to retrieve a jewel that lay buried in the heart of an infamous dragon, and the fifth was asked to bring back a cowry-shell born from swallows.

For years, the five men ventured across the known world to compete their quests. The first nobleman eventually realised the impossible nature of his task and forged the bowl, before presenting it to Lady Kaguya. She took the bowl from him, but when night came she saw that it did not glow with holy light and, realising that the nobleman had tried to deceive her, told him he had failed in his quest.

The second nobleman also tried to forge the golden branch he had been asked to retrieve, but he too was found out. The third and fourth noblemen fared no better and, eventually realizing the folly of their pursuit, gave up on their quests, while the fifth, in search of the strange cowry-shell, lost his life in a far off land.

News of Lady Kaguya eventually reached the Emperor and he sent one of his maids to meet with this mysterious young woman. Lady Kaguya, however, refused to meet with the Emperor's messenger. The Emperor then sent a letter to the bamboo cutter and his daughter, inviting them to his palace, and offering to bestow a noble title upon the old man. The bamboo cutter was overjoyed by the offer, but his happiness faded when he saw the look on his daughter. Lady Kaguya looked at him sadly, and explained that if she ever left his house she would die.

So the bamboo cutter travelled to the palace alone, and explained the situation to the Emperor. Intrigued by this enigmatic young lady, the Emperor decided to pay her a visit and so he travelled back with the bamboo cutter.

When they stepped inside his house, the Emperor saw Lady Kaguya. Her back was turned to him, and she was bathed in a wondrous glow. But when she turned and caught his gaze, she disappeared before his very eyes. The Emperor looked around bewildered and called her name, pleading with her to return.

And so she did.

At once the Emperor declared his undying love for this mysterious stranger, but Lady Kaguya explained once more, that if she left the house she would die. And so, with a heavy heart, the Emperor eventually left.

In time the Bamboo cutter and his wife noticed a change that gradually came over their daughter, she became quiet and pensive, and whenever she looked up at the full moon her eyes would fill with tears. At first she would not answer when asked if anything was wrong, but eventually, in an outpouring of grief, she explained that she was not of the Earth at all, but from the Moon, and that soon some of her fellow Moon People would come to take her back to the place of her birth.

Mystified, her father asked her why she had come to Earth. Lady Kaguya explained that there had been a great war on her world, and that she had been sent to Earth for her own safety. Now that the war was over, she would have to go home.

The Emperor soon heard this story, and fearing that he would lose her forever, he sent his personal guards to stop her from being taken away.

The guards waited for many days, and on the night of the next full Moon, a brilliant cloud descended from the heavens. It was so bright that the guards were almost blinded and rendered helpless. Within the cloud there were many Moon People, who descended from a strange craft. The Moon People approached the bamboo cutter's house, and ordered that Lady Kaguya return with them to their world.

Lady Kaguya knew there was no possibility of her staying on Earth, and so she stepped out of the house with her parents. A Moon Man handed her a bottle containing an Elixir of Immortality, and she took a deep gulp of the magical liquid. She apologized to her mother and father, and asked them to forgive her for causing them such pain.

She wrote a tearful message and handed it to the Emperor's most faithful guard, and asked that it, and the remains of the Elixir, be taken to the man who loved her more than anyone.

A Moon Man handed her a robe of feathers, which she put over her shoulders, and as she did so, all the sadness that had filled her heart disappeared – along with all her memories of the Earth, the Emperor and her parents. Then she ascended the steps into the craft, and set off with the other Moon People to their homeland.

The guard delivered the letter and the Elixir. The Emperor read how Lady Kaguya had wanted to be with him, that it pained her greatly to leave Earth, that their union was forbidden, and that she had to return to the Moon.

Upon finishing the letter, the Emperor was overcome with sadness. He turned to one of his courtiers and asked, "Which mountaintop is closest to heaven?"

He was told that it was a mountain in the Suruga Province. The Emperor handed the letter and Elixir to his most faithful guard, and asked him to take them to the top of the mountain and burn them both.

Upon seeing the stunned expressions of his courtiers, the Emperor explained that he did not want to drink the Elixir and become immortal, and remain forever with the thought that he would never see Lady Kaguya again.

So his men climbed to the top of the highest known mountain and carried out his orders. And to this day people still see smoke rising from the Mountain of Immortality, or Mount Fuji, and watch as the fumes become as one with the clouds of heaven.

The Man in the Moone

Francis Godwin

Introduction

Francis Godwin (1562–1633) was the Bishop of
Llandaff, and son of Thomas Godwin, Bishop of Bath
and Wells. *The Man in the Moone* was an influential
piece written in the late 1620s, and published
posthumously in 1638.

In this fanciful tale the narrator, Domingo Gonsales,
tells how he used a flock of birds to take him to the
Moon. Here he discovers that the citizens of the Moon
are Christians who live in a Utopian paradise. This
book was influenced by the astronomers Johannes
Kepler and Galileo Galilei, and physicist William
Gilbert.

In this version, edited for Firestone Books, the
spelling and punctuation have been modernized, and
some minor amendments have been made. (For
instance Francis Godwin uses the term "Gansas" for
swans. Gansa is actually Spanish for goose, and the
plural is not "Gansas" but gansos. In this version we
have simply used the term "swan".)

Written in a time where spellings had not been
standardized, some words were originally written by
Francis Godwin with modern American spellings (e.g.
favor, center, etc) while others have modern English
spellings (e.g. colour); these have neither been
Anglicized or Americanized but left as they are. Also

the spelling of the title has not been changed, as the book is still best-known as *The Man in the Moone*.

A glossary has also been included at the back of the book. This is well worth referencing before reading the tale, as the story does contain archaic and foreign-language words that may otherwise be confusing.

The narrator states more than once that he will recount more of his lunar adventures in a second book which, it appears, was never written.

This enjoyable, fantastical tale has influenced numerous books, in a lineage that goes right through to Jules Verne and beyond. It was parodied in Cyrano de Bergerac's 1657 novel *The Comical History of the States and Empires of the Moon* (a portion of which is included in the second volume of the *Early Science Fiction* series). It also influenced Aphra Behn's play *The Emperor of the Moon*. It is also possible that *The Man in the Moone*, via *The Comical History*, influenced *Gulliver's Travels* by Jonathan Swift.

It is referenced in the notes of *The Unparalleled Adventure of One Hans Pfaall* by Edgar Allan Poe (also available in the second volume of the *Early Science Fiction* series), which in turn is referenced in Jules Verne's classic science fiction tale *From the Earth to the Moon*.

THE MAN IN THE MOONE:

OR
A Discourse Of A Voyage thither
BY
DOMINGO GONSALES
The Speedy Messenger

LONDON
Printed by JOHN NORTON
1638

To the Ingenious Reader.

Thou hast here an essay of Fancy, where Invention is showed with Judgement. It was not the Author's intention (I presume) to discourse thee into a belief of each particular circumstance. 'Tis fit thou allow him a liberty of conceit; where thou takest to thy self a liberty of judgement. In substance thou hast here a new discovery of a new world, which perchance may find little better entertainment in thy opinion, than that of Columbus at first, in the esteem of all men. Yet his then but poor espial of America, betrayed unto knowledge so much as hath since increased into a vast plantation. And the then-unknown, is now of as large an extent as all the then-known world.

That there should be Antipodes was once thought as great a Paradox as now that the Moon should be habitable. But the knowledge of this may seem more properly reserved for this our discovering age: In which our Galileos, can by advantage of their spectacles gaze the Sun into spots, & descry mountains in the Moon. But this, and more in the ensuing discourse I leave to thy candid censure, & the faithful relation of the little eye-witness, our great discoverer.

E. M.

The Man in the Moone

Francis Godwin

'Tis well enough and sufficiently known to all the countries of Andalucia, that I, Domingo Gonsales, was borne of Noble parentage, and that in the renowned City of Seville, to wit in the year 1552, my Father's name being Therrando Gonsales, (that was near kinsman by the Mother's side unto Don Pedro Sanchez, that worthy Count of Almenara) and, as for my Mother, she was the daughter of the Reverend and famous Lawyer, Otho Perez de Salaveda, Governor of Barcelona, and Corrigidor of Biscay.

Being the youngest of 17 Children they had, I was put to school, and intended by them unto the Church. But our Lord purposing to use my service in matters of far other nature and quality, inspired me with spending some time in the wars. It was at the time that Don Fernando, the Noble and thrice renowned Duke D'Alva, was sent into the Low Countries, viz. the year of Grace 1568.

I then, following the current of my aforesaid desire, leaving the University of Salamanca, (whither my Parents had sent me) without giving knowledge unto any of my dearest friends, got me through France, unto Antwerp, where in the month of June 1569, I arrived in some poor state. For having sold my Books and

Bedding, with such other stuff as I had, which happily yielded me some 30 ducats, and borrowed of my Father's friends some 20 more, I bought me a little nag with which I travelled more thriftily than young Gentlemen are wont ordinarily to do, until at last arriving within a league of Antwerp, certain of the cursed Guises set upon me, and bereaved me of Horse, money, and all, whereupon I was fain (through want and necessity) to enter into the service of Marshal Cossey, a French Nobleman, whom I served truly in honourable place, although mine enemies gave it out to my disgrace that I was his horse-keeper's boy. But for that matter I shall refer myself unto the report of the Count Mansfield, Monsieur Tavier, and other men of known worth and estimation, who have often testified unto many of good credit yet living, the very truth in that behalf, which indeed is this:

Monsieur Cossey, who about that time had been sent as Ambassador unto the Duke D'Alva, Governor of the Low Countries, he I say, understanding the Nobility of my birth, and my late misfortune, thinking it would be no small honour to him, to have a Spaniard of that quality about him, furnished me with horse, armour, and whatsoever I wanted, using my service in nothing so much (after once I had learned the French tongue) as writing his Letters, because my hand indeed was then very fair. In the time of war, if upon necessity I now and then dressed mine own Horse, it ought not to be cast in my teeth, seeing I hold it the part of a Gentleman, for setting forward the service of his Prince, to submit himself unto the vilest office.

The first expedition I was in, was against the Prince of Orange, at what time the Marshal my friend aforesaid, met him making a road into France, and putting him to flight, chased him even unto the walls of Cambrai. It was my good hap at that time to defeat a horseman of the enemy, by killing his Horse with my pistol, which falling upon his leg, so as he could not stir, he yielded himself to my mercy, but I knowing mine own weakness of body, and seeing him a lusty, tall fellow, thought it my surest way to dispatch him, which having done, I rifled him of a chain, money, and other things to the value of 200 ducats.

No sooner was that money in my purse, but I began to resume the remembrance of my nobility, and giving unto Monsieur Cossey the besa los manos, I got myself immediately unto the Duke's court, where were divers of my kindred, that (now they saw my purse full of good Crowns) were ready enough to take knowledge of me. By their means I was received into pay, and in process of time obtained a good degree of favour with the Duke, who sometimes would jest a little more broadly at my personage than I could well brook. For although I must acknowledge my stature to be so little, as no man there is living, I think, less, yet in as much as it was the work of God, and not mine, he ought not to have made that a means to dishonour a Gentleman withal. And those things which have happened unto me, may be an example, that great and wonderful things may be performed by most unlikely bodies, if the mind be good, and the blessing of our Lord do second and follow the endeavours of the same.

Well, howsoever the Duke's merriments went against my stomach, I framed myself the best I could to dissemble my discontent, and by such my patience accommodating myself also unto some other his humors, so wan his favour, as at his departure home into Spain, (whither I attended him) the year 1573 by his favour and some other accidents, (I will say nothing of my own industry, wherein I was not wanting to myself) I was able to carry home in my purse the value of 3000 Crowns.

At my return home, my Parents, who were marvellously displeased with my departure, received me with great joy, and the rather, for that they saw I brought with me means to maintain myself without their charge, having a portion sufficient of mine own, so that they needed not to deduct anything from my brothers or sisters for my setting up.

But fearing I would spend it as lightly as I got it, they did never leave importuning me, till I must needs marry the daughter of a Portuguese, a Merchant of Lisbon, a man of great wealth and dealings, called John Figueres. Therein I satisfied their desire, and putting not only my marriage money, but also a good part of mine own Stock into the hands of my father-in-law, or such as he wished me unto, I lived in good sort, even like a Gentleman, with great content for divers years.

At last it fell out, that some disagreement happened between me and one Pedro Delgades, a Gentleman of my kin, the causes whereof are needless to be related, but so far this dissension grew between us, as when no mediation of friends could appease the same, into the field we went together alone with our Rapiers, where my chance was to kill him, being a man of great strength, and tall stature. But what I wanted of him in strength, I supplied with courage, and my nimbleness more than countervailed his stature.

This fact being committed in Carmona, I fled with all the speed I could to Lisbon, thinking to lurk with some friend of my father-in-law's, till the matter might be compounded, and a course taken for a sentence of Acquittal by consent of the prosecutors. This matter fell out in the year 1596, even at that time that a certain great Count of ours came home from the West-Indies, in triumphant manner, boasting and sending out his declarations in print, of a great victory he had obtained against the English, near the Isle of Pines. Whereas the truth is, he got of the English nothing at all in that Voyage, but blows and a great loss.

Would to God that Lying and Vanity had been all the faults he had, his covetousness was like to be my utter undoing, although since it hath proved a means of eternizing my name for ever with all Posterity, (I verily hope) and to the unspeakable good of all mortal men, that in succeeding ages the world shall have if at the leastwise it may please God that I do return safe home again into my Country, to give perfect instructions how those admirable devices, and past all credit of possibility, which I have lit upon, may be imparted unto public use.

You shall then see men to fly from place to place in

the air; you shall be able (without moving or travelling of any creature) to send messages in an instant many Miles off, and receive answer again immediately; you shall bee able to declare your mind presently unto your friend, being in some private and remote place of a populous City, with a number of such like things: but that which far surpasseth all the rest, you shall have notice of a new World, of many most rare and incredible secrets of Nature, that all the Philosophers of former ages could never so much as dream off.

But I must be advised, how I be over-liberal, in publishing these wonderful mysteries, till the Sages of our State have considered how far the use of these things may stand with the Policy and good government of our Country, as also with the Fathers of the Church, how the publication of them, may not prove prejudicial to the affairs of the Catholic faith and Religion, which I am taught (by those wonders I have seen above any mortal man that hath lived in many ages past) with all my best endeavours to advance, without all respect of temporal good, and so I hope I shall.

But to go forward with my narration: so it was that the bragging Captain, above named, made a show of his great discontentment, for the death of the said Delgades was indeed some kin to him. Howbeit he would have been entreated, so that I would have given him no less than one thousand Ducats (for his share) to have put up his Pipes, and surceased all suite in his Kinsman's behalf; I had by this time, besides a wife, two sons whom I liked not to beggar by satisfying the desire of this covetous braggart and the rest, and therefore constrained of necessity to take another course.

I put myself in a good Carrack that went for the East Indies, taking with me the worth of two thousand Ducats to traffic withal, being yet able to leave so much more for the estate of my wife and children, whatsoever might become of me and the goods I carried.

In the Indies I prospered exceedingly well, bestowing my stock in Jewels, namely, for the most part in Diamonds, Emeralds, and great Pearls, of which I had such pennyworths, as my stock being safely returned to Spain, (so I heard it was) must needs yield ten for one.

But myself upon my way homeward soon after we had doubled the East of Buena Speranza, fell grievously sick for many days, making account by the same sickness to end my life, as undoubtedly I had done, had we not (even then as we did) recovered that same blessed Isle of St. Helena, the only paradise, I think, that the Earth yieldeth, of the healthfulness of the Air there, the fruitfulness of the soil, and the abundance of all manner of things necessary for sustaining the life of man, what should I speak, seeing there is scant a boy in all Spain, that hath not heard of the same?

I cannot but wonder, that our King in his wisdom hath not thought fit to plant a Colony, and to fortify in it, being a place so necessary for refreshing of all travellers out of the Indies, as it is hardly possible to make a Voyage thence, without touching there.

It is situated in the Altitude of sixteen degrees to the South, and is about three leagues in compass, having no firm land or continent within three hundred leagues; nay not so much as an Island within one hundred leagues of the same, so that it may seem a miracle of Nature, that out of so huge and tempestuous an Ocean, such a little piece of ground should arise and discover itself.

Upon the South side there is a very good harbour, and near unto the same divers edifices built by the Portingals to entertain passengers, amongst the which there is a pretty Chapel, handsomely beautified with a Tower, having a fair Bell in the same. Near unto this housing there is a pretty Brook of excellent fresh water, divers fair walks made by hand, and set along upon both sides, with Fruit-Trees, especially Oranges, Lemons, Pomegranates, Almonds, and the like, which bear Fruit all the year long, as do also the Fig-Trees, Vines, Pear-Trees (whereof there are divers sorts,) Palmitos, Cocos, Olives, Plums. Also I have seen there such as we call Damaxælas, but few. As for Apples I dare say there are none at all. Of garden Herbs there is good store, as of Parsley, Cole-worts, Rosemary, Melons, Gourds, Lettuce, and the like. Corn likewise growing of itself, incredible plenty, as Wheat, Peas, Barley, and almost all kinds of Pulse, but chiefly it aboundeth with Cattle, and Fowl, as Goats, Swine, Sheep, and Horses, Partridges, wild Hens, Pheasants, Pigeons, and wild Fowl, beyond all credit: especially there are to be seen about the Months of February, and March, huge flocks of a certain kind of wild Swans (of which I shall have cause hereafter to speak more) that like our Cuckoos, and Nightingales, at a certain season of the year, do vanish away, and are no more to be seen.

On this blessed Island did they set me ashore with a Negro to attend me, where, praised be God, I recovered my health, and continued there for the space of one whole year, solacing myself (for lack of humane society) with Birds, and brute beasts. As for Diego (so was the Black Moor called) he was constrained to live at the West end of the Island, in a Cave, because being always together, victuals would not have fallen out so plenty. If the Hunting or Fowling of the one had succeeded well, the other would find means to invite him, but if it were scant with both, we were fain both to bestir ourselves. Marry that fell out very seldom, for no creatures there do any whit more fear a man, than they do a Goat or Cow.

By reason thereof, I found means easily to make tame divers sorts both of Birds and Beasts, which I did in a short time, only by muzzling them, so till they came either unto me, or else Diego, they could not feed.

At first I took great pleasure in a kind of Partridge, of which I made great use, as also of a tame Fox. For when soever I had any occasion to confer with Diego, I would take me one of them, being hungry, and tying a note about his neck, beat him from me, whereupon straight they would away to the Cave of Diego, and if they found him not there, still would they beat up and down all the West end of the Island, till they had hunted him out. Yet this kind of conveyance not being without some inconvenience, needless here to be recited, after a certain space I persuaded Diego (who though he were a fellow of good parts, was ever content to be ruled by me) to remove his habitation unto a promontory or cape upon the North-West part of the Island, being, though a league off, yet within sight of my house and Chapel, and then, so long as the weather was fair, we could at all times, by signals, declare our minds to each other in an instant, either by night, or by day, which was a thing I took great pleasure in.

If in the night season I would signify anything to him, I used to set up a light in the Tower or place where our bell hung. It is a pretty large room, having a fair window, well-glassed, and the walls within being plastered, were exceedingly white. By reason thereof, though the light were but small, it gave a great show, as also it would have done much further off if need had been.

This light after I had let stand some half-hour, I used to cover, and then, if I saw any signal of light again from my companion at the cape, I knew that he waited for my notice, which perceiving, by hiding and showing my light, according to a certain rule and agreement between us, I certified him at pleasure what I list. The like course I took in the day to advertise him of my pleasure, sometimes by smoke, sometimes by dust, sometimes by a more refined and more effectual way.

But this Art containeth more mysteries than are to

be set down in few words. Hereafter I will perhaps afford a discourse for it of purpose, assuring myself that it may prove exceedingly profitable unto mankind, being rightly used and well-employed, for that which a messenger cannot perform in many days, this may dispatch in a piece of an hour. Well, I notwithstanding after a while grew weary of it, as being too painful for me, and betook me again to my winged messengers.

Upon the Seashore, especially about the mouth of our River, I found great store of a certain kind of wild Swan (before mentioned) feeding almost altogether upon the prey, and (that which is somewhat strange) partly of Fish partly of Birds, having (which is also no less strange) one foot with Claws, talons, and pounces, like an Eagle, and the other whole like a Swan or water fowl.

These birds using to breed there in infinite numbers, I took some thirty or forty young ones of them, and bred them up by hand partly for my recreation, partly also as having in my head some rudiments of that device, which afterwards I put in practise. These being strong and able to continue a great flight, I taught them first to come at call afar off, not using any noise but only the show of a white Cloth. And surely in them I found it true that phrase delivered by Plutarch, how that *Animalia Carnivora*, they are *dociliora quam alterius cuiusvis generis*. It were a wonder to tell what tricks I had taught them, by that time they were a quarter year old. Amongst other things I used them by little and little to fly with burdens, wherein I found them able, above all credit, and brought them to that pass, as that a white sheet being displayed unto them by Diego upon the side of a hill, they would carry from me unto him, Bread, flesh, or any other thing I list to send, and upon the like call return unto me again.

Having prevailed thus far, I began to cast in my head how I might do to join a number of them together in bearing of some great burden which, if I could bring to pass, I might enable a man to fly and be carried in the air, to some certain place safe and without hurt. In this cogitation having much laboured my wits and made some trial, I found by experience that if many were put to the bearing of one great burden, by reason it was not possible all of them should rise together just in one instant. The first that raised himself upon his wings, finding himself stayed by a weight heavier than he could move or stir, would by and by give over, as also would the second, third, and all the rest. I devised therefore at last a means how each of them might rise, carrying but his own proportion of weight only, and it was thus.

I fastened about every one of my Swans a little pulley of Cork, and putting a string through it of meetly length, I fastened the one end thereof unto a block almost of eight Pounds weight, unto the other end of the string I tied a poise, weighing some two Pounds, which being done, and causing the signal to be erected, they presently rose all (being four in number) and carried away my block unto the place appointed. This falling out according to my hope and desire, I made proof afterwards, but using the help of two or three birds more, in a Lamb, whose happiness I much envied, that he should be the first living creature to take possession of such device.

At last after divers trials I was surprised with a great longing, to cause myself to be carried in the like sort. Diego, my Moor, was likewise possessed with the same desire, and but that otherwise I loved him well, and had need of his help, I should have taken that his ambitious affection in very evil part, for I hold it far more honour to have been the first flying man, than to be another Neptune that first adventured to sail upon the Sea.

Howbeit not seeming to take notice of the mark he aimed at, I only told him (which also I take to be true) that all my Swans were not of sufficient strength to carry him, being a man, though of no great stature, yet twice my weight at least.

So upon a time having provided all things necessary I placed myself, with all my trinkets, upon the top of a rock at the River's mouth, and putting myself at full Sea upon an Engine (the description whereof ensueth) I caused Diego to advance his Signal, whereupon my Birds presently arose, twenty-five in number, and carried me over lustily to the other rock on the other side, being about a Quarter of a league.

The reason why I chose that time and place, was that I thought somewhat might perchance fall out in this enterprise contrary to my expectation, in which case I assured myself the worst that could be, was but to fall into the water where, being able to swim well, I hoped to receive little or no hurt in my fall. But when I was once over in safety, O how did my heart even swell with joy and admiration of mine own invention! How often did I wish myself in the midst of Spain, that speedily I might fill the world with the fame of my glory and renown? Every hour I wished with great longing for the Indian Fleet to take me home with them, but they stayed (by what mischance I know not) three Months beyond the accustomed time.

At last they came being in number three Carracks sore weather-beaten, their people being for the most part sick and exceedingly weak, so as they were constrained to refresh themselves in our Island one whole month.

The Captain was called Alphonso de Xima, a Valiant man; wise, and desirous of renown, and worthy of better fortune than afterwards befell him. Unto him I opened the device of my Swans, well knowing how impossible it were otherwise to persuade him to take in so many Birds into the Ship, that would be more troublesome, for the niceness of provision to be made for them, than so many men. Yet I adjured him by all manner of Oaths, and persuasions, to afford me both true dealing, and secrecy. Of the last I doubted not much, as assuring myself, he would not dare to impart the device to any other, before our King were acquainted with it. Of the first I feared much more, namely, lest Ambition and the desire of drawing unto himself the honour of such an invention, should cause him to make me away. Yet I was forced to run the hazard, except I would adventure the loss of my Birds, the like whereof for my purpose were not to be had in all Christendom, nor any that I could be sure, would ever serve the turn.

Well, that doubt in proof fell out to be causeless. The man, I think, was honest of himself, but had he dealt treacherously with me, I had laid a plot for the discovery of him, as he might easily judge I would, which peradventure somewhat moved him, yet God knows how he might have used me, before my arrival in Spain, if in the mean course we had not been intercepted, as you shall hear.

Upon Thursday the twenty-first of June, to wit in the year 1599, we set sail towards Spain. I having allowed me a very convenient Cabin for my Birds, and stowage also for mine Engine, which the Captain would have had me leave behind, and it is a marvel I had not, but my good fortune therein saved my life, and gave me that which I esteem more than a hundred lives, if I had them. For thus it fell out: After two Months' sail, we encountered a fleet of the English, some ten leagues from the Island of Tenerife, one of the Canaries, which is famous through the World for a Hill upon the same called El Pico, that is to be discerned and kenned upon the Sea no less than one hundred leagues off.

We had aboard us five times the number of people they had, we were well provided of munition, and our men in good health. Yet seeing them disposed to fight, and knowing what infinite riches we carried with us, we thought it a wiser way to fly, if we might, than by encountering a company of dangerous fellows to hazard not only our own lives, which a man of valour in such a case esteemeth not, but the estates of many poor Merchants, who I am afraid were utterly undone by miscarriage of that business. Our fleet then consisted of five ships, to wit: three Carracks, a Barque, and a Caravel, that coming from the Isle of Saint Thomas had, in an evil hour for him, overtaken us some few days before.

The English had three Ships, very well appointed, and no sooner spied, but they began to play for us and changing their course, as we might well perceive, endeavoured straight away to bring us under their lee, which they might well do (as the wind stood) especially being light nimble vessels, and yare of Sail, as for the most part all the English shipping is, whereas ours was heavy, deep-laden, and foul with the Sea. Our Captain therefore resolved peradventure wisely enough, but I am sure neither valiantly nor fortunately, to flee, commanding us to disperse ourselves.

The Caravel, by reason of too much haste, fell foul upon one of the Carracks, and bruised her so, as one of the English that had undertaken her, easily fetched her up and entered her. As for the Caravel she sank immediately in the sight of us all.

The Barque (for ought I could perceive) no man making after her, escaped unpursued, and another of our Carracks, after some chase, was given over by the English, that making account to find a booty good enough of us, and having us between them and their third company, made upon us with might and main. Wherefore our Captain that was aboard us, gave direction to run aland upon the Isle, the Port whereof we could not recover, saying that he hoped to save some of the goods, and some of our lives, and the rest he had rather should be lost, than commit all to the mercy of the enemy.

When I heard of that resolution, seeing the Sea to work high, and knowing all the coast to be full of blind rocks, and Shoals, so as our Vessel might not possibly come near land, before it must be rent in a thousand pieces, I went unto the Captain, showing him the desperateness of the course he intended, wishing him rather to try the mercy of the enemy, than so to cast away himself, and so many brave men. But he would not hear me by any means, whereupon discerning it to be high time to shift for myself, first, I sought out my Box or little Casket of stones, and having put it into my sleeve, I then betook me to my Swans, put them upon my Engine, and myself upon it, trusting (as indeed it happily fell out) that when the Ship should split, my Birds, although they wanted their Signal, of themselves, and for safeguard their own lives (which nature hath taught every living creature to preserve to their power) would make towards the Land, which fell out well (I thank God) according to mine expectation.

The people of our Ship marvelled about what I went, none of them being acquainted with the use of my Birds, but the Captain. For Diego was in the Rosaria, the Ship that fled away unpursued (as before I told you).

Some half a league we were from the Land, when our Carrack struck upon a rock, and split immediately, whereupon I let loose unto my Birds the reins, having first placed myself upon the highest of the Deck. And with the shock they all arose, carrying me fortunately unto the Land, whereof, whether I were well apaid you need not doubt, but a pitiful sight it was unto me, to behold my friends and acquaintances in that miserable distress of whom notwithstanding many escaped better than they had any reason to hope for. For the English launching out their Cockboats, like men of more noble, and generous disposition than we are pleased to esteem them, taking compassion upon them, used all the diligence they could, to help such as had any means to save themselves from the fury of the waves, and that even with their own danger amongst many, they took up our Captain, who (as Father Pacio could since tell me) having put himself into his Cockboat with twelve others, was induced to yield himself unto one Captain Raymond, who carried him together with our Pilot along in their voyage with them, being bound for the East Indies.

But their hard hap was by a breach of the Sea near the cape of Buena Esperanza, to be swallowed of the merciless Waves, whose fury a little before they had so hardly escaped. The rest of them, as I likewise heard, and they were in all some twenty-six persons that they took into their ship, they set them aland soon after at Cape Verde.

As for myself, being now ashore in a Country inhabited for the most part by Spaniards, I reckoned myself in safety. Howbeit I quickly found the reckoning, I so made, mine Host had not been acquainted with all. For it was my chance to pitch upon that part of the Isle, where the hill, before mentioned, beginneth to rise. And it is inhabited by a Savage kind of people, that live upon the sides of that hill, the top whereof is always covered with Snow, and held for the monstrous height and steepness not to be accessible either for man or beast.

Howbeit these Savages fearing the Spaniards, (between whom and them there is a kind of continual war) hold themselves as near the top of that hill as they can, where they have divers places of good strength, never coming down into the fruitful Valleys, but to prey upon what they can find there.

It was the chance of a company of them to espy me within some hours space after my Landing. Thinking they had lit upon a booty, made towards me with all the speed they could, but not so privily as that I could not perceive their purpose before they came near to me by half a quarter of a League; seeing them come down the side of a Hill with great speed directly towards me, divers of them carrying Long Staves, besides other weapons, which because of their distance from me I might not discern, I thought it high time to bestir me and shift for myself, and by all means to keep myself out of the fingers of such slaves who, had they caught me, for the hatred they bear to us Spaniards, would have surely hewed me all to pieces.

The Country in that place was bare, without the coverture of any wood. But the mountain before spoken of, beginning even there to lift up itself, I espied in the side of the same, a white cliff which I trusted my Swans would take for a signal, and being put off, would make all that way, whereby I might quickly be carried so far, as those barbarous Cullions should not be able to overtake me, before I had recovered the dwelling of some Spaniard, or at leastwise might have time to hide myself from them, till that in the night, by help of the stars, I might guide myself toward Las Læguna, the City of that Island, which was about one league off, as I think.

Wherefore with all the celerity that might be, I put myself upon mine Engine and let loose the reins unto my Swans. It was my good fortune that they took all one way, although not just that way I aimed at.

But what then, O Reader? Prepare thy self unto the hearing of the strangest Chance that ever happened to any mortal man, and that I know thou wilt not have the Grace to believe, till thou seest it seconded with Iteration of Experiments in the like, as many a one, I trust, thou mayest in short time.

My Swans, like so many horses that had gotten the bit between their teeth, made not towards the cliff I aimed at, although I used my wonted means to direct the Leader of the flock that way, but with might and main took up towards the top of El Pico, and did never stay till they came there: a place where they say never man came before, being in all estimation at least fifteen leagues in height perpendicularly upwards above the ordinary level of the Land and Sea.

What manner of place I found there, I should gladly relate unto you, but that I make hast to matters of far greater Importance. There when I was set down, I saw my poor Swans fall to panting and blowing, gaping for breath as if they would all presently have died; wherefore I thought it not good to trouble them awhile, forbearing to draw them in, which they never wont to endure without struggling, and little expecting that which followed.

It was now the season that these Birds were wont to take their flight away, as our Cuckoos and Swallows do in Spain towards the Autumn. They, as after I perceived, mindful of their usual voyage, even as I began to settle myself for the taking of them in, as it were with one consent, rose up, and having no other place higher to make toward, to my unspeakable fear and amazement, struck bolt upright, and never did lin towering upward, and still upward, for the space, as I might guess, of one whole hour, toward the end of which time, me thought I might perceive them to labour less and less; till at length, O incredible thing, they forebear moving anything at all! and yet remained unmoveable, as steadfastly as if they had been upon so many perches.

The Lines slacked. Neither I, nor the Engine moved at all, but abode still as having no manner of weight. I found then by this Experience that which no Philosopher ever dreamed of, to wit, that those things which we call heavy do not sink toward the Center of the Earth, as their natural place, but as drawn by a secret property of the Globe of the Earth, or rather something within the same, in like sort as the Loadstone draweth Iron, being within the compass of the beams attractive.

For though it be true that there they could abide

unmoved without the prop or sustentation of any corporal thing other than the air, as easily and quietly as a fish in the middle of the water, yet forcing themselves never so little, it is not possible to imagine with what swiftness and celerity they were carried, and whether it were upward, downward, or sidelong, all was one.

Truly, I must confess, the horror and amazement of that place was such, as if I had not been armed with a true Spanish courage and resolution, I must needs have died there with very fear. But the next thing that did most trouble me, was the swiftness of Motion, such as did even almost stop my breath. If I should liken it to an Arrow out of a Bow, or to a stone cast down from the top of some high tower, it would come far short, and short.

Another thing there was exceedingly, and more than exceedingly troublesome unto me, and that was the Illusions of Devils and wicked spirits, who, the first day of my arrival, came about me in great numbers, carrying the shapes and likeness of men and women, wondering at me like so many Birds about an Owl, and speaking divers kinds of Languages which I understood not, till at last I did light upon them that spake very good Spanish, some Dutch, and others Italian, for all these Languages I understood.

And here I saw only a touch of the Sun's absence for a little while once, ever after having him in my sight. Now to yield you satisfaction in the other. You shall understand that my Swans, although entangled in my lines, might easily find means to seize upon divers kinds of Flies and Birds, as especially Swallows and Cuckoos, whereof there were multitudes, as Motes in the Sun. Although to say the truth I never saw them to feed anything at all. As for myself, I was much beholding unto those same, whether Men or Devils I know not, that amongst divers speeches, which I will forbear a while to relate, told me, that if I would follow their directions, I should not only be brought safely to my home, but also be assured to have the command of all pleasures of that place, at all times.

To the which motions not daring to make a flat denial, I prayed a time to think of it, and withal entreated them (though I felt no hunger at all, which may seem strange) to help me with some victuals, lest in the meanwhile I should starve. They did so, readily enough, and brought me very good Flesh and Fish of divers sorts, well-dressed but that it was exceedingly fresh and without any manner of relish or salt.

I also tasted wine there of divers sorts, as good as any in Spain, and Beer no better in all Antwerp. They wished me then, while I had means to make my provision, telling me, that till the next Thursday they could not help me to any more, if happily then, at what time also they would find means to carry me back and set me safe in Spain where I would wish to be, so that I would become one of their fraternity, and enter into such covenants and profession as they had made to their Master and Captain, whom they would not name. I answered them gently for the time, telling them, I was very glad of such an offer, praying them to be mindful of me as occasion served.

So for that time I was rid of them, having first furnished my Pockets with as much Victual as I could thrust in, amongst the which I failed not to afford place for a little Bottle of good Canary wine.

Now shall I declare unto you the quality of the place, in which I then was. The Clouds I perceived to be all under me, between me and the Earth. The stars, by reason it was always day, I saw at all times alike, not shining bright, as upon the Earth we are wont to see them in the night time, but of a whitish Colour, like that of the Moon in the daytime with us. And such of them as were to be seen (which were not many) I showed far greater than with us, yea, no less than ten times so great. As for the Moon being then within two days of the change, she appeared of a huge and fearful quantity.

This also is not to be forgotten, that no stars appeared but on that part of the Hemisphere that was next the Moon, and the nearer to her the bigger in Quantity they appeared. Again I must tell you, that whether I lay quiet and rested, or else were carried in the air, I perceived myself still to be always directly between the Moon and and the Earth. Whereby it appeareth, not only that my Swans took none other way than directly toward the Moon, but also, that when we rested, as at first we did for many hours, either we were insensibly carried (for I perceived no such motion) round about the Globe of the Earth, or else that, according to the late opinion of Copernicus, the Earth is carried about, and turneth round perpetually, from West to the East, leaving unto the

Planets only that motion which Astronomers call natural, and is not upon the Poles of the Equinoctial, commonly termed the Poles of the World, but upon those of the Zodiac. Concerning which question, I will speak more hereafter, when I shall have leisure to call to my remembrance the Astronomy that I learned being a young man at Salamanca, but have now almost forgotten.

The air in that place I found quiet without any motion of wind, and exceedingly temperate, neither hot nor cold, as where neither the Sunbeams had any subject to reflect upon, neither was yet either the Earth or water so near as to affect the air with their natural quality of coldness. As for that imagination of the Philosophers, attributing heat together with moistness unto the air, I never esteemed it otherwise than a fancy. Lastly now it is to be remembered that after my departure from the Earth, I never felt any appetite of hunger or thirst. Whether the purity of the air, our proper element not being infected with any Vapors of the Earth and water might yield nature sufficient nutriment, or what else might be the cause of it, I cannot tell, but so I found it, although I perceived myself in perfect health of body, having the use of all my limbs and senses; and strength both of body and mind, rather beyond and above, than anything short of the pitch, or wonted vigour. Now let us go on, and we shall go more than apace.

Not many hours after the departure of that devilish company from me, my Swans began to bestir themselves, still directing their course toward the

Globe or body of the Moon, and they made their way with that incredible swiftness, as I think they gained not so little as Fifty Leagues in every hour. In that passage I noted three things very remarkable: one that the further we went, the lesser the Globe of the Earth appeared unto us; whereas still on the contrary side the Moon showed her self more and more monstrously huge.

Again, the Earth, which ever I held in mine eye, did, as it were, mask itself with a kind of brightness like another Moon; and even as in the Moon we discerned certain spots or Clouds, as it were, so did I than in the Earth. But whereas the form of those spots in the Moon continue constantly one and the same, these little and little did change every hour. The reason thereof I conceive to be this: that whereas the Earth according to her natural motion, (for that such a motion, she hath, I am now constrained to join in opinion with Copernicus) turneth round upon her own Axis every twenty-four hours from the West unto the East. I should at the first see in the middle of the body of this new star a spot like unto a Pear that had a morsel bitten out upon one side of him. After certain hours, I should see that spot slide away to the East side. This no doubt was the main of Africa.

Then should I perceive a great shining brightness to occupy that room, during the like time (which was undoubtedly none other than the great Atlantic Ocean). After that succeeded a spot almost of an Oval form, even just such as we see America to have in our Maps. Then another vast clearness representing the West

Ocean; and lastly a medley of spots, like the Countries of the East Indies. So that it seemed unto me no other than a huge Mathematical Globe, leisurely turned before me, wherein successively, all the Countries of our Earthly world within the compass of twenty-four hours were represented to my sight. And this was all the means I had now to number the days and take reckoning of time.

Philosophers and Mathematicians should now confess the wilfulness of their own blindness. They have made the world believe hitherto that the Earth hath no motion. And to make that good they are fain to attribute unto all and every of the celestial bodies, two motions quite contrary to each other; whereof one is from the East to the West, to be performed in 24 hours (that they imagine to be forced, *per raptum primi Mobilis*) the other from the West to the East in several proportions.

O incredible thing, that those same huge bodies of the fixed stars in the highest orb, whereof divers are by themselves confessed to be more than one hundred times as big as the whole Earth, should as so many nails in a Cartwheel be whirled about in that short space, whereas it is many thousands of years (no less, I trow, they say, than thirty-thousand) before that orb do finish his Course from West to East, which they call the natural motion.

Now whereas to every of these they yield their natural course from West to East, therein they do well. The Moon performeth it in twenty-seven days; the Sun, Venus, and Mercury in a year or thereabouts;

Mars in three years; Jupiter in twelve years, and Saturn in thirty.

But to attribute unto these celestial bodies contrary motions at once, was a very absurd conceit, and much more, to imagine that same Orb wherein the fixed stars are, whose natural course taketh so many thousand of years, should every 24 hours be turned about. I will not go so far as Copernicus, that maketh the Sun the Center of the system, and unmoveable. Neither will I define anything one way or other. Only this I say, allow the Earth his motion (which these eyes of mine can testify to be his due) and these absurdities are quite taken away, every one having his single and proper Motion only.

But where am I? At the first I promised a History, and I fall into disputes before I am aware. There is yet one accident more befell me worthy of especial remembrance: that during the time of my stay I saw, as it were, a kind of cloud of a reddish colour growing toward me, which continually growing nearer and nearer, at last I perceived to be nothing else but a huge swarm of Locusts.

He that readeth the discourses of learned men, concerning them, and namely that of John Leo in his description of Africa, how that they are seen in the air many days before they fall upon a country, adding unto that which they deliver, this experience of mine will easily conclude that they cannot come from any other place than the Globe of the Moon.

But give me leave now at last to pass on my journey quietly, without interruption for Eleven or Twelve days, during all which time I was carried directly toward the Globe or body of the Moon with such a violent whirling as cannot be expressed.

For I cannot imagine that a bullet out of the mouth of a Cannon could make way through the vaporous and muddy air near the Earth with that celerity, which is most strange, considering that my Swans moved their wings but even now and then, and sometimes not at all in a Quarter of an hour together. Only they held them stretched out, so passing on as we see that Eagles and Kites sometimes will do for a little space, when (as one speaks, I remember) *contabundo volatu pene eodem locopendula circum ventur*; and during the time of those pauses I believe they took their naps and times of sleeping; for other (as I might easily note) they had none.

Now for myself: I was so fast knit unto my Engine, as I durst commit myself to slumbering enough to serve my turn, which I took with as great ease (although I am loath to speak it, because it may seem incredible) as if I had been in the best Bed of down in all Antwerp.

After Eleven days' passage in this violent flight, I perceived that we began to approach near unto another Earth, if I may so call it, being the Globe or very body of that star which we call the Moon.

The first difference that I found between it and our Earth, was that it showed itself in his natural colours. Ever after I was free from the attraction of the Earth, whereas with us, a thing removed from our eye but a league or two, begins to put on that lurid and deadly colour of blue.

Then, I perceived also that it was covered for the most part with a huge and mighty Sea, those parts only being dry Land, which show unto us here somewhat darker than the rest of her body (that I mean which the Country people call *el hombre della Luna*, the Man of the Moon).

As for that part which shineth so clearly in our eyes, it is even another Ocean, yet besprinckled here and there with Islands, which for the littleness so far off we cannot discern.

So that fame splendor appearing unto us, and giving light unto our night, appeareth to be nothing else but the reflection of the Sunbeams returned unto us out of the water, as out of a glass. How ill this agreeth with that which our Philosophers teach in the schools, I am not ignorant.

But alas how many of their Errors hath time and experience refuted in this our age, with the recital whereof I will not stand to trouble the reader. Amongst many other of their vain surmises, the time and order of my narration putteth me in mind of one which now my experience found most untrue. Who is there that hath not hitherto believed the uppermost Region of the air to be extreme hot, as being next forsooth unto the natural place of the Element of Fire.

O Vanities, Fancies, Dreams!

After the time I was once quite free from the attractive Beams of that tyrannous Loadstone the Earth, I found the air of one and the self same temper, without Winds, without Rain, without Mists, without

Clouds, neither hot nor cold, but continually after one and the same tenor, most pleasant, mild, and comfortable, till my arrival in that new World of the Moon.

As for that Region of Fire our Philosophers talk of, I heard no news of it; mine eyes have sufficiently informed me there can be no such thing.

The Earth by turning about had now showed me all her parts twelve times when I finished my course. For when by my reckoning it seemed to be (as indeed it was) Tuesday the Eleventh day of September, at what time the Moon being two days old was in the Twentieth degree of Libra, my Swans stayed their course as it was with one consent, and took their rest for certain hours, after which they took their flight, and within less than one hour, let me upon the top of a very high hill in that other world, where immediately presented unto mine eyes many most strange sights.

For first I observed, that although the Globe of the Earth showed much bigger there than the Moon doth unto us, even to the full trebling of her diameter, yet all manner of things there was of largeness, and quantity, ten, twenty, I think I may say thirty times more than ours.

Their trees at least three times so high as ours, and more than five times the breadth and thickness. So their herbs, Beasts, and Birds, although to compare them with ours I know not well how, because I found not anything there, any species either of Beast or Bird that resembleth ours at all, except Swallows, Nightingales, Cuckoos, Woodcocks, Bats, and some kinds of wild Fowl, as also of such Birds as my Swans, all which, (as now I well perceived,) spend the time of their absence from us, even there in that world; neither do they vary anything at all either in quantity or quality from those of ours here, as being none other than the very same, and that not only specie, but number. But of these novelties more hereafter in their due places.

No sooner was I let down upon the ground, But I was surprised with a most ravenous hunger, and earnest desire of eating. Wherefore, stepping unto the next tree, I fastened thereunto my Engine, with my Swans, and in great haste fell to searching of my pockets for the Victuals I had reserved as aforesaid. But to my great amazement and discomfort, I found instead of Partridge and Capon which I thought to have put there, a mingle mangle of dry leaves, of Goat's hair, Sheep or Goat's dung, Moss, and such like trash.

As for my Canary Wine, it was turned to a stinking and filthy kind of liquor like the Urine of some Beast. O, the illusions of wicked spirits, whose help if I had been fain only to rely upon – you see how I had been served.

Now while I stood musing and wondering at this strange Metamorphosis, I heard my Swans upon the sudden to make a great fluttering behind me. And looking back, I espied them to fall greedily upon a certain shrub within the compass of their lines, whose leaves they fed upon most earnestly, where heretofore, I had never seen them to eat any manner of green meat whatsoever. Whereupon stepping to the shrub, I put a leaf of it between my teeth. I cannot express the pleasure I found in the taste thereof, such it was I am sure, as if I had not with great discretion moderated my appetite, I had surely surfeited upon the same.

In the mean time it fell out to be a bait that well contented both my Birds and me at that time, when we had need, of some good refreshing.

Scarcely had I ended this banquet, when upon the sudden I saw myself environed with a kind of people most strange, both for their feature, demeanour, and apparel. Their stature was most divers, but for the most part, twice the height of ours: their colour and countenance most pleasing, and their habit such, as I know not how to express.

For neither did I see any kind of Cloth, Silk, or other stuff to resemble the matter of that whereof their Clothes were made. Neither, which is most strange, of all other, can I devise how to describe the colour of them, being in a manner all clothed alike.

It was neither black, nor white, yellow, nor red, green, nor blue, nor any colour composed of these. But if you ask me what it was then, I must tell you: it was a colour never seen in our Earthly world, and therefore neither to be described unto us by any, nor to be conceived of one that never saw it. For as it were a hard matter to describe unto a man borne blind the difference between blue and green, so can I not bethink myself any means how to decipher unto you this Lunar colour, having no affinity with any other that ever I beheld with mine eyes. Only this I can say of it, that it was the most glorious and delightful, that can possibly be imagined. Neither in truth was there any one thing that more delighted me, during my abode in that new world, than the beholding of that most pleasing and resplendent colour.

It remaineth now that I speak of the Demeanour of this people, who presenting themselves unto me upon the sudden and that in such extraordinary fashion as I have declared, being struck with a great amazement, I crossed myself, and cried out: "Jesus, Maria!"

No sooner was the word "Jesus" out of my mouth, but young and old fell all down upon their knees, at which I not a little rejoiced, holding up both their hands on high and repeating all certain words which I understood not.

Then presently, they all arising, one that was far the tallest of them came unto me and embraced me with great kindness, and giving order (as I partly perceived) unto some of the rest to stay by my Birds. He took me by the hand, and leading me down toward the foot of the hill, brought me to his dwelling, being more than half a league from the place where I first alighted.

It was such a building for beauty and hugeness, as all our world cannot show anything comparable to it. Yet such I saw afterwards elsewhere, as this might seem but a Cottage in respect of them.

There was not a door about the house, that was not thirty foot high, and twelve in breadth. The rooms were between forty and fifty foot in height, and so all other proportions answerable. Neither could they well be much less, the Master inhabiting them, being full twenty-eight foot high.

As for his corporature, I suppose verily that if we had him here in this world to be weighed in the balance, the poise of his body would show itself more ponderous than Five and Twenty, peradventure thirty of ours.

After I had rested myself with him the Value of one of our days, he led me some Five leagues off, unto the Palace of the Prince of the Country.

The stateliness of the building whereof I will leave unto the second part of this work, as also many other particulars which will minister more pleasure to the reader, than yet I may afford him, being desirous in this first part to set down no more than what the process of my story concerning my Journey doth necessarily draw from me.

This Prince whose stature was much higher than the former, is called (as near as I can by Letters declare it, for their sounds are not perfectly to be expressed by our Characters) Pylonas, which signifieth in their Language, First, if perhaps it be not rather a denotation of his dignity and authority, as being the prime Man in all those parts – In all those parts, I say – for there is one supreme Monarch amongst them, of stature yet much more huge than he, commanding over all that whole Orb of that world, having under him twenty-nine other Princes of exceedingly great power, and every of them twenty-four others, whereof this Pylonas was one.

The first ancestor of this great Monarch came out of the Earth (as they deliver) and by marriage with the inheritrix of that huge Monarchy, obtaining the government, left it unto his posterity, who ever since have held the same, even for the space of forty-thousand days or Moons, which amounteth unto three-thousand and seventy-seven Years.

And his name being Irdonozur, his heiress, unto this day, do all assume unto themselves that name, he, they say, having continued there well near four-hundred Moons, and having begotten divers children returned (by what means they declare not) unto the Earth again. I doubt not but they may have their Fables, as well as we.

And because our Histories afford no mention of any Earthly man to have ever been in that world before myself, and much less to have returned thence again, I cannot but condemn that tradition for false and fabulous. Yet this I must tell you, that learning seemeth to be in great estimation among them, and that they make semblance of deterring all Lying and falsehood, which is wont there to be severely punished.

Again, which may yield some countenance unto their historical narrations, many of them live wonderful long, even beyond all credit, to wit even unto the age as they professed unto me of thirty-thousand Moons, which amounteth unto a thousand years and Upwards (so that the ages of three or four, men might well reach unto the time of the first Irdonozur). And this is noted generally: that the taller people are of Stature, the more excellent they are for all endowments of mind, and the longer time they do live.

For whereas (that which before I partly intimated unto you) their stature is most diverse, great numbers of them little exceedingly ours; such seldom live above the age of a thousand Moons, which is answerable to eighty of our years. And they account them most base creatures, even but a degree before brute beasts, employing them accordingly in all the basest and most servile offices, terming them by a word that signifieth bastard men, counterfeits, or Changelings, so those whom they account Genuine, natural, and true Lunars, both in quantity of body and length of life, they have for the most part thirty times as much as we, which proportion agreeth well with the quantity of the day in both worlds, theirs containing almost thirty of ours.

Now, when I declare unto you the manner of our travel unto the Palace of Pylonas, you will say you scarce ever heard anything more strange and incredible. Unto every one of us there was delivered at our first setting forth, two Fans of Feathers, not much unlike to those that our Ladies do carry in Spain, to make a cool air unto themselves in the heat of Summer. The use of which Fans before I declare unto you, I must let you understand that the Globe of the Moon is not altogether destitute of an attractive Power, but it is so far weaker than that of the Earth, as if a man do but spring upward, with all his force, (as Dancers do when they show their activity by capering) he shall be able to mount fifty or sixty foot high, and then he is quite beyond all attraction of the Moon, falling down no more, so as by the help of these Fans, as with wings, they convey themselves in the air in a short space (although not with that swiftness that Birds do) even whither they list.

In two hours space (as I could guess) by the help of these fans, wee were carried through the air those five Leagues; being about sixty persons. Being arrived at the Palace of Pylonas, after our conductor had gotten audience (which was not presently) and had declared what manner of present he had brought, I was immediately called in unto him by his attendance. The stateliness of his Palace, and the reverence done unto him, I soon discerned his greatness, and therefore framed myself to win his favour the best I might.

You may remember I told you of a certain little Box or Casket of Jewels, the remainder of those which being brought out of the East Indies, I sent from Isle of St. Helena into Spain. These before I was carried in unto him I took out my pocket in a corner, and making choice of some of every sort, made them them ready to be presented as I should think fit.

I found him sitting in a most magnificent chair of Estate, having his Wife or Queen upon one hand, and his eldest son on the other, which both were attended, the one by a troop of Ladies, and the other of young men, and all along the side of the room stood a great number of goodly personages, whereof scarce any one was lower of statute than Pylonas, whose age they say is now twenty-one thousand Moons.

At my first entrance falling down upon my knees, I thought good to use unto him these words in the Latin tongue: "Propitius sit tibi Princeps Illustrissime Dominus noster Jesus Christus, etc."

As the people I first met withal, so they hearing the holy name of our Saviour they all, I say, King, Queen, and all the rest fell down upon their knees, pronouncing a word or two I understood not. They being risen again I proceeded thus: "Et Maria Salvatoris Genetrix, Petrus et Paulus, etc."

And so reckoning up a number of Saints, to see if there were anyone of them that they honoured as their patron, at last reckoning among others St. Martinus, they all bowed their bodies, and held up hands in sign of great reverence, the reason whereof I learned to be, that Martin in their language signifieth God. Then taking out my Jewels, prepared for that purpose, I presented unto the King or Prince (call him how you please) seven stones of so many several sorts: a Diamond, a Ruby, an Emerald, a Sapphire, a Topaz, a Turquoise and an Opal, which he accepted with great joy and admiration, as having not often seen any such before.

Then I offered unto the Queen and Prince some other, and was about to have bestowed a number of more, upon other there present, but Pylonas forbade them to accept, thinking, as afterwards I learned, that they were all I had, and being willing they should be reserved for Irdonozur, his Sovereign.

This done, he embraced me with great kindness, and began to inquire of me divers things by signs, which I likewise answered by signs as well as I could. But not being able to give him content, he delivered me to a guard of a hundred of his Giants (so I may well call them) commanding straightly: First that I should want nothing that might be fit for me; Secondly that they should not suffer any of the dwarf Lunars (if I may so term them) to come near me; Thirdly that I should with all diligence to be instructed in their Language. And lastly, that by no means they should impart unto me, the knowledge of certain things particularly by him specified, marry what those particulars were, I might never by any means get knowledge.

It may be now you will desire to understand what were the things Pylonas inquired of me. Why what but these? Whence I came, how I arrived there, and by what means? What was my name? What my Errand? and such like. To all which I answered the very truth as near as I could.

Being dismissed, I was afforded all manner of necessaries that my heart could wish, so as it seemed unto me I was in a very Paradise, the pleasures whereof notwithstanding could not so overcome me, as that the remembrance of my Wife and Children did not trouble me much.

And therefore being willing to foster any small spark of hope of my return, with great diligence, I took order for the attendance of my Swans whom myself in person tended every day with great carefulness, all of which notwithstanding had fallen out to little purpose, had not other men's care performed that which no endeavour of mine own could.

For the time now approached, when of necessity all the people of our stature (and so myself among the rest) must needs sleep for some thirteen or fourteen whole days together.

So it commeth to pass there by a secret power, and unresistable decree of nature, that when the day beginneth to appear and the Moon to be enlightened by the Sunbeams (which is at the first Quarter of the Moon) all such people as exceed not very much our stature inhabiting those parts, they fall into a dead sleep, and are not possibly to be wakened till the Sun be set, and withdrawn out of their sight, even as Owls, and Bats, with us cannot endure the light, so we there at the first approach of the day, begin to be amazed with it, and fall immediately into a slumber, which groweth by little and little, into a dead sleep, till this light depart from thence again, which is not in fourteen or fifteen days, to wit, until the last quarter.

Me thinks now I hear some man to demand what manner of light there is in that world during the absence of the Sun, to resolve you for that point, you shall understand that there is a light of two sorts.

One of the Sun (which I might not endure to behold) and another of the Earth. That of the Earth was now at the highest, for that when the Moon is at the Change, then is the Earth (unto them in the Moon) like a full Moon with us, and as the Moon increaseth with us, so the light of the Earth decreaseth with them. I then found the light there (though the Sun were absent) equal unto that with us, in the day time, when the Sun is covered with clouds, but toward the quarter it little and little diminisheth, yet leaving still a competent light, which is somewhat strange.

But much stranger is that which was reported unto me there: how that in the other Hemisphere of the Moon (I mean contrary to that which I happened upon) where during half the Moon, they see not the Sun, and the Earth never appeareth unto them. They have, notwithstanding, a kind of light (not unlike by their description to our Moonlight) which it seemeth the propinquity of the stars and other Planets (so much near unto them than us) affordeth.

Now you shall understand that of the true Lunars there be three degrees:

Some beyond the pitch of our stature a good deal, as perhaps ten or twelve foot high, that can endure the day of the Moon, when the Earth shineth but little, but not endure the beams of both, at such time they must be content to be laid asleep.

Others there are of twenty foot high, or somewhat more, that in ordinary places endure all light both of Earth and Sun. Marry there is a certain Island, the mysteries whereof none may know whose stature is at least twenty-seven foot high (I mean of the measure of the Standard of Castile). If any other come aland there in the Moon's daytime, they fall asleep immediately. This Island they call God's Island, or Insula Martini in their language. They say it hath a particular Governor, who is, as they report, of age sixty-five thousand Moons, which amounteth to five thousand of our years. His name is said to be Hiruch, and he comandeth after a fort over Irdonozur himself, especially in that Island out of which he never commeth.

There is another repairing much thither, they say is half his age and upwards, to wit, about thirty-three thousand Moons, or twenty-six hundred of our years, and he commandeth in all things, throughout the whole Globe of the Moon, concerning matters of Religion, and the service of God, as absolutely as our holy Father the Pope doth in any part of Italy. I would fain have seen this man, but I might not be suffered to come near him. His name is Imozes.

Now give me leave to settle myself to a long night's sleep: My attendants take charge of my Birds, prepare my lodging, and signify to me by signs, how it must be with me. It was about the middle of September, when I perceived the air to grow more clear than ordinary, and with the increasing of the light, I began to feel myself first dull, then heavy and willing to sleep, although I had not lately been hindered from taking mine ease that way.

I delivered myself at last into the custody of this sister of Death, whose prisoner I was for almost a fortnight after. Awaking then, it is not to be believed how fresh, how nimble, how vigorous, I found all the faculties both of my body and mind.

In good time, therefore, I settled myself immediately to the learning of the language which (a marvellous thing to consider) is one of the same throughout all the regions of the Moon, yet so much the less to be wondered at, because I cannot think all the Earth of Moon to Amount to the fortieth part of our inhabited Earth; partly because the Globe of the Moon is much less than that of the Earth, and partly because their Sea or Ocean covereth in estimation Three parts of Four (if not more), whereas the superficies of our land may be judged Equivalent and comparable in Measure to that of our Seas.

The Difficulty of that language is not to be conceived, and the reasons thereof are especially two: First, because it hath no affinity with any other that ever I heard. Secondly, because it consisteth not so much of words and Letters, as of tunes and uncouth sounds, that no letters can express.

For you have few words but they signify diverse and several things, and they are distinguished only by their tunes that are as it were sung in the utterance of them. Yea many words there are consisting of tunes only, so as if they list they will utter their minds by tunes without words. For Example, they have an ordinary salutation amongst them, signifying (Verbatim), "Glory be to God alone," which they express (as I take it, for I am no perfect Musician) by a tune without any words at all. Yea the very names of Men they will express in the same sort.

By occasion hereof, I discern means of framing a Language (and that easy soon to be learned) as copious as any other in the world, consisting of tunes only, whereof my friends may know more at leisure if it please them.

This is a great Mystery and worthier the searching after than at first sight you would imagine. Now notwithstanding the difficulty of this language, within two Months space I had attained unto such knowledge of the same, as I understand most questions to be demanded of me, and what with signs, what with words, make reasonable shift to utter my mind, which thing being certified unto Pylonas, he sent for me oftentimes, and would be pleased to give me knowledge of many things that my Guardians durst not declare unto me.

Yet this I will say of them, that they never abused me with any untruth that I could perceive, but if I asked a question that they liked not to resolve me in, they would shake their heads and with a Spanish shrug pass over to other talk.

After seven Months' space it happened that the great Irdonozur, making his progress to a place some two hundred leagues distant from the Palace of Pylonas, sent for me. The History of that Journey, and the conference that passed between us shall be related at large in my second book. Only thus much thereof at this time, that he would not admit me into his presence, but talked with me through a Window, where I might hear him, and he both hear and see me at pleasure.

I offered him the remainder of my Jewels, which he accepted very thankfully, telling me that he would requite them with gifts of another manner of value.

It was not above a Quarter of a Moon that I stayed there, before I was sent back unto Pylonas again, and so much the sooner, because if we had stayed but a day or two longer, the Sun would have overtaken us, before we could have recovered our home.

The gifts he bestowed on me were such as a Man would forsake mountains of Gold for, and they were all stones, to wit nine in number, and those of three sorts, whereof one they call Poleastis another Machrus, and third Ebelus, of each sort three.

The first are of the bigness of an Hazelnut, very like unto jet, which among many other incredible virtues hath this property that being once heat in the Fire, they ever after retain their heat (though without any appearance) until they be quenched with some kind of liquor, whereby they receive no detriment at all, though they be heat and quenched ten thousand times. And their heat is so vehement, as they will make redhot any metal that shall come within a foot of them, and being put in a Chimney, shall make a room as warm, as if a great Fire were kindled in the same.

The Machrus (yet far more precious than the other) is of the colour of Topaz, so shining and resplendent, as (though not past the bigness of a bean) being placed in the midst of a large Church in the night time, it maketh it all as light, as if a hundred Lamps were hanged up round about it.

Can you wish for properties in a stone of greater use than these? Yes my Ebelus will afford you that which I dare say will make you prefer him before these, yea and all the Diamonds, Sapphires, Rubies, and Emeralds that our world can yield, were they laid in a heap before you, to say nothing of the colour, (the Lunar whereof I made mention before, which notwithstanding is so incredibly beautiful, as a man should travel a thousand Leagues to behold it). The shape is somewhat flat of the breadth of a Pistole, and twice the thickness. The one side of this which is somewhat more Orient of Colour than the other, being clapped to the bare skin of a man, in any part of his body, it taketh away from it all weight or ponderousness, whereas turning the other side it addeth force unto the attractive beams of the Earth, either in this world or that, and maketh the body to weigh half so much again as it did before.

Do you marvel now why I should so over-prize this stone? Before you see me on Earth again, you shall understand more of the value of this kind and invaluable Gem.

I inquired then amongst them, whether they had not any kind of Jewel or other means to make a man invisible, which me thought had been a thing of great and extraordinary use. And I could tell that divers of our learned men had written many things to that purpose.

They answered that if it were a thing feasible, yet they assured themselves that God would not suffer it to be revealed to us creatures subject to so many imperfections, being a thing so apt to be abused to ill purposes, and that was all I could get of them.

Now after it was known that Irdonozur, the great Monarch, had done me this honour, it is strange how much all men respected me more than before. My Guardians, which hitherto were very nice in relating anything to me concerning the government of that world, now became somewhat more open, so as I could learn (partly of them and partly of Pylonas) what I shall deliver unto you concerning that matter. Whereof I will only give you a taste at this time, referring you unto a more ample discourse in my second part, which at my return into Spain you shall have at large, but not till then for causes heretofore related.

In a thousand years it is not found that there is either Whore-monger amongst them, whereof these reasons are to be yielded:

There is no want of anything necessary for the use of man.

Food groweth everywhere without labour, and that of all sorts to be desired.

For raiment, housing, or anything else that you may imagine possible for a man to want, or desire, it is provided by the command of Superiors, though not without labour, yet so little, as they do nothing but as it were playing, and with pleasure.

Again their Females are all of an absolute beauty, and I know not how it commeth to pass by a secret disposition of nature there, that a man having once known a Woman, never desireth any other.

As for murder it was never heard of amongst them; neither is it a thing almost possible to be committed, for there is no wound to be given which may not be cured, they assured me (and I for my part do believe it) that although a man's head be cut off, yet if any time within the space of Three Moons it be put together, and joined to the Carcass again, with the appointment of the Juice of a certain herb, there growing, it will be joined together again, so as the party wounded shall become perfectly whole in a few hours.

But the chief cause, is that through an excellent

disposition of that nature of people there, all, young and old, do hate all manner of vice, and do live in such love, peace, and amity, as it seemeth to be another Paradise. True it is, that some are better disposed than others, but that they discern immediately at the time of their birth.

And because it is an inviolable decree amongst them never to put any one to death, perceiving by the stature, and some other notes they have, who are likely to be of a wicked or imperfect disposition, they send them away (I know not by what means) into the Earth, and change them for other children, before they shall have either ability or opportunity to do amiss among them. But first, they say, they are fain to keep them there for a certain space, till that the air of the Earth may alter their colour to be like unto ours.

And their ordinary vent for them is a certain high hill in the North of America, whose people I can easily believe to be wholly descended of them, partly in regard of their colour, partly also in regard, of the continual use of Tobacco which the Lunars use exceedingly much, as living in a place abounding wonderfully with moisture, as also for the pleasure they take in it, and partly in some other respects too long now to be rehearsed.

Sometimes they mistake their aim, and fall upon Christendom, Asia or Africa, marry that is but seldom. I remember some years since, that I read certain stories tending to the confirmation of these things delivered by these Lunars, as especially one Chapter of William of Newburgh's *De Rebus Anglicis*. It is towards the end of his first book, but the chapter I cannot particularly resign.

Then see Inigo Mondejar in his description of New Granada, the second book; as also Joseph Desia de Carana, in his history of Mexico. If my memory fails me not, you will find in these, that which will make my report much the more credible. But for testimonies I care not.

May I once have the happiness to return home in safety, I will yield such demonstrations of all I deliver, as shall quickly make void all doubt of the truth hereof.

If you will ask me further of the manner of government amongst the Lunars, and how Justice is executed, alas what need is there of Exemplary punishment, where there are no offences committed? They need there no Lawyers, for there is never any contention, the seeds thereof, if any begin to sprout, being presently by the wisdom of the next superior pulled up by the roots.

And as little need is there of Physicians, they never misdirect themselves, their air is always temperate and pure, neither is there any occasion at all of sickness, as to me it seemed at least, for I could not hear that ever any of them were sick.

But the time that nature hath assigned unto them being spent, without any pain at all they die, or rather (I should say) cease to live, as a candle to give light, when that which nourisheth it is consumed.

I was once at the departure of one of them, which I wondered much to behold, for notwithstanding the happy life he led, and multitude of friends and children he should forsake, as soon as certainly he understood and perceived his end to approach, he prepared a great feast, and calling about him all those he especially esteemed of, he bids them be merry and rejoice with him, for that the time was come he should now leave the counterfeit pleasures of that world, and be made partaker of all true joys and perfect happiness.

I wondered not so much at his constancy, as the behaviour of those his friends. With us in the like case, all seem to mourn, when often some of them do but laugh in their sleeves, or as one says under a vizard.

They all on the other side, young and old, both seemingly, and in my conscience, sincerely did rejoice thereat, so as if any dissembled, it was but their own grief conceived for their own particular loss.

Their bodies being dead putrify not, and therefore are not buried but kept in certain rooms ordained for that purpose, so as most of them can show their Ancestors bodies uncorrupt for many generations.

There is never any rain, wind, or change of the air, never either Summer, or Winter, but as it were a perpetual Spring, yielding all pleasure, all content, and that free from any annoyance at all.

O, my Wife and Children, what wrong have you done me to bereave me of the happiness of that place, but it maketh no matter, for by this voyage am I sufficiently assured, that ere long the race of my mortal life being run, I shall attain a greater happiness elsewhere, and that everlasting.

It was the Ninth day of September that I began to

ascend from El Pico; twelve days I was upon my Voyage, and arrived in that Region of the Moon, that they call Simiri, September the twenty-first following.

The twelfth day of May being Friday, we came unto the Court of the great Irdonozur, and returned back the Seventeenth unto the Palace of Pylonas. There I continued till the month of March, in the year 1601, at what time I earnestly besought Pylonas (as I had often done before) to give me leave to depart, (though with never so great hazard of my life) back into the Earth again.

He much dissuaded me, laying before me the danger of the voyage, the misery of that place from whence I came, and the abundant happiness of that I now was in. But the remembrance of my Wife and Children over-weighed all these reasons, and to tell you the truth, I was so far forth moved with a desire of that deserved glory, that I might purchase at my return, as methought I deserved not the name of a Spaniard, if I would not hazard twenty lives, rather than loose but a little possibility of the same.

Wherefore I answered him, that my desire of seeing my Children was such, as I knew I could not live any longer, if I were once out of hope of the same. When then he desired one year's stay longer, I told him it was manifest I must depart now or never; My Birds began to droop, for want of their wonted migration, three of them were now dead and, if a few more failed, I was for ever destitute of all possibility of returning.

With much ado, at last he condescended unto my request, having first acquainted great Irdonozur with my desire then, perceiving by the often baying of my Birds, a great longing in them to take their flight, I trimmed up mine Engine, and took my leave of Pylonas, who (for all the courtesy he had done me) required of me but one thing, which was faithfully to promise him, that if ever I had means thereunto, I should salute from him Elizabeth, whom he termed the great Queen Of England, calling her the most glorious of all women living, and indeed he would often question with me of her, and therein delighted so much, as it seemed he was never satisfied in talking of her. He also delivered unto me a token or present for her of no small Value. Though I account her an enemy of Spain, I may not fail of performing this promise as soon as I shall be able so to do, upon the twenty-ninth day of March being Thursday, three days after my awakening from the last Moon's light, I fastened myself to mine Engine, not forgetting to take with me, besides the Jewels Irdonozur had given me (with whose use and virtues Pylonas had acquainted me at large) a small quantity of Victual, wherefore afterward I had great use as shall be declared.

An infinite multitude of people (and amongst the rest Pylonas himself) being present, after I had given him the last besa los manos, I let loose the rains unto my Birds, who with great greediness taking wing quickly, carried me out of their sight. It fell out with me as in my first passage, I never felt either hunger or thirst, till I arrived in China upon a high mountain, some five Leagues from the high and mighty City of Pachin.

This Voyage was performed in less than nine days. I heard no news by the way of these airy men, which I had seen in my ascending. Nothing stayed my journey any whit at all, whether it was the earnest desire of my Birds to return to the Earth, where they had missed one season, or that the attraction of the Earth so much stronger than that of the Moon, furthered their labour, so it came to pass, although now I had three Birds wanting of those I carried forth with me.

For the first eight days my Birds flew in front, and I, with the Engine, was as it were drawn by them. The Ninth day, when I began to approach unto the Clouds, I perceived myself and mine Engine to sink towards the Earth, and go before them.

I was then horribly afraid, lest my Birds not being able to bear our weight, they being so few, should be constrained to precipitate both me and themselves headlong to the Earth: wherefore I thought it no less than needful to make use of the Ebelus (one of the stones bestowed upon me by Irdonozur) which I clapped to my bare flesh within my hose, and it appeared manifestly thereupon unto me that my Birds made their way with much greater ease than before, as being lightened of a great burden. Neither do I think it possible for them to have let me down safely unto the Earth without that help.

China is a Country so populous, as I think there is hardly a piece of ground to be found (in the most barren parts of the same) though but thrice a man's length, which is not most carefully manured.

I being yet in the air, some of the country people

had espied me, and came running unto me by troops, they seized upon me, and would needs, by and by, carry me unto an Officer. I seeing no other remedy, yielded myself unto them. But when I assayed to go, I found myself so light, that I had much ado, one foot being upon the ground, to set down the other, that was by reason of my Ebelus so applied, as it took quite away all weight and ponderousness from my body. Wherefore bethinking myself what was to be done, I feigned a desire of performing the necessity of nature, which by signs being made known unto them (for they understood not a word of any Language I could speak) they permitted me to go aside among a few bushes, assuring themselves that for me to escape from them it was impossible. Being there I remembered the directions Pylonas had given me concerning the use of my stones, and first I took them all together, with a few Jewels yet remaining of those I had brought out of India, and knit them up in my handkerchief; all, except one the least and worst Ebelus.

Him I found means to apply in such sort unto my body, as but the half of his side touched my skin, whereby it came to pass that my body then had but half the weight, that being done I drew towards these my Guardians, till seeing them come somewhat near together they could not cross my way, I showed them a fair pair of heels. This I did to the end I might recover an opportunity of finding my Stones and Jewels, which I knew they would rob me off, if I prevented them not.

Being thus lightened, I bid them such a chase, as

had they been all upon the backs of so many Zebras, they could never have overtaken me. I directed my course unto a certain thick wood, into which I entered some a quarter of a League, and then finding a pretty spring (which I took for my mark) hard by it, I thrust my Jewels into a little hole made by a Mole, or some such like creature.

Then I took out of my pocket my Victuals, to which in all my Voyage I had not till then any desire, and refreshed myself therewith, till such time as the people pursuing me, had overtaken me, into whose hands I quietly delivered myself.

They led me unto a mean Officer, who (understanding that once I had escaped from them that first apprehended me) caused a certain feat to be made of boards, into which they closed me in such sort, as only my head was at liberty, and then carried me upon the shoulders of four slaves (like some notorious malefactor) before a man of great authority, whom in their language as after I learned, they called a Mandarin, abiding two days journey off, to wit one League distant from the great and famous City of Pachin, or Paquin, by the Chinese called Suntien.

Their language I could no way understand; only this I could discern, that I was for something or other accused with a great deal of vehemence.

The substance of this accusation, it seems, was that I was a Magician, as witnessed my strange carriage in the air. That being a stranger, as appeared by my both language and habit I, contrary to the Laws of China, entered into the Kingdom without warrant, and that probably with no good intent.

The Mandarin heard them out, with a great deal of composed gravity, and being a man of quick apprehension, and withal studious of novelties, he answered them that he would take such order with me, as the case required, and that my bold attempt should not want its deserved punishment.

But having dismissed them he gave order to his Servants, that I should be kept in some remote parts of his vast Palace, and be strictly watched, but courteously used. This do I conjecture, by what at the present I found, and what after followed. For my accommodation was every way better, than I could expect. I lodged well and was treated well, and could not fault anything, but my restraint.

In this manner did I continue many Months, afflicted with nothing so much as with the thought of my Swans, which I knew must be irrecoverably lost, as indeed they were. But in this time, by my own industry, and the forwardness of those that accompanied me, I was grown indifferent ready in the ordinary language of that Province (for almost every Province in China, hath its proper Language) whereat I discerned they took no small content, I was at length to take the air, and brought into the spacious garden of that Palace, a place of excellent pleasure and delight, as being planted with Herbs and Flowers of admirable both sweetness and beauty, and almost infinite variety of fruits, both European and others, and all those composed with that rare curiosity that I was ravished with the contemplation of such delightful objects.

But I had not here long recreated myself, yet the Mandarin entered the Garden, on that side where I was walking, and being advertised thereof by his servants, and wished to kneel down unto him (as I after found it to be the usual public reverence to those great Officers). I did so, and humbly craved his favour towards a poor stranger, that arrived in those parts, not by his own destination, but by the secret disposal of the heavens.

He in a different language (which all the Mandarins, as I have since learned, do use) and that like that of the Lunars did consist much of tunes, but was by one of his servants interpreted to me. He, I say, wished me to be of good comfort, for that he intended no harm unto me, and so passed on.

The next day I was commanded to come before him, and so conducted into a sumptuous dining room exquisitely painted and adorned. The Mandarin, having commanded all to avoid the room, vouchsafed conference with me in the vulgar language, inquiring first the estate of my Country, the power of my Prince, the religion and manners of the people, wherein being satisfied by me, he at last descended to the particulars of my education and studies, and what brought me into this remote country. Then did I at large declare unto him the adventure of my life, only omitting, here and there, what particulars I thought good, forbearing especially any mention of the stones given me by Irdonozur.

The strangeness of my story did much amaze him. And finding in all my discourse nothing any way tending to Magic (wherein he had hoped by my means to have gained some knowledge) he began to admire the excellence of my wit, applauding me for the happiest man that this world had ever produced and, wishing me to repose myself after my long narration, he for that time dismissed me.

After this, the Mandarin took such delight in me, that no day passed, wherein he sent not for me. At length he advised me to apparel myself in the habit of the Country (which I willingly did) and gave me not only the liberty of his house, but took me also abroad with him, when he went to Paquin, whereby I had the opportunity by degrees to learn the disposition of the people, and the policy of the Country, which I shall reserve for my second part.

Neither did I by this my attendance on him gain only the knowledge of these things, but the possibility also of being restored to my native soil, and to those dear pledges which I value, above the world, my Wife and Children.

For by often frequenting Paquin, I at length heard of some Fathers of the Society that were become famous for the extraordinary favor by the King vouchsafed them, to whom they had presented some European trifles, as Clocks, Watches, Dials, and the like, which with him passed for exquisite rarities. To them, by the Mandarins leave, I repaired. I was welcomed by them; they much wondering to see a Lay Spaniard there, whither they had with so much difficulty obtained leave to arrive.

There did I relate to Father Pantoja and those others

of the society these fore-related adventures, by whose directions I put them in writing, and sent this story of my fortunes to Macao, from thence to be conveyed for Spain, as a forerunner of my return. And the Mandarin being very indulgent unto me, I came often unto the Fathers, with whom I consulted about many secrets with them also did I lay a foundation for my return, the blessed hour whereof I do with patience expect; that by enriching my Country with the knowledge of hidden mysteries, I may once reap the glory of my fortunate misfortunes.

FINIS

Glossary

Aland On the land

Antipodes Places on Earth that are diametrically opposite each other (e.g. the poles)

Apaid Pleased

Assayed Attempted

Bait Food

Barque A sailing ship. The term has the same root as the word Barge

Besa los manos A kiss of the hand when bidding farewell

Caravel A fifteenth century Portuguese ship

Carrack A three or four-masted ship first built in the fifteenth century

Celerity Swiftness

Corporature Physique

Coverture Covering

Cullion An unpleasant person (from "Coillon" a French word for testicle)

Divers Many

Espial Observation

Fain Willingly

Forsooth Truly

Inheritrix Female inheritor

Lin Cease

List Desired

Marry But surely

Peradventure Perhaps

Pistole A Spanish coin

Portingals Portuguese

Raiment Clothing

Space Duration

Superficies Surface

Surcease Cease

Sustentation To sustain

Trow Think or Believe

Victuals Food

Vizard Mask or visor

Whore-monger Fornicator

Yare Quick

For more information on the latest publications please visit:

www.firestonebooks.com

You can also find out more by following us on Facebook and Twitter